THE
TWO-THOUSAND-POUND
GOLDFISH

**Other APPLE® PAPERBACKS
by Betsy Byars:**

The Cybil War
Goodbye, Chicken Little
The Pinballs
Trouble River
The TV Kid

**And still more APPLE® PAPERBACKS
you will want to read:**

Blackbird Singing
   by Eve Bunting
*The Revenge of the Incredible Dr. Rancid
and His Youthful Assistant, Jeffrey*
   by Ellen Conford
Mr. Wolf and Me
   by Mary Francis Shura
The Secret of NIMH
(hardcover title: Mrs. Frisby and the Rats of NIMH)
   by Robert C. O'Brien
Son for a Day
   by Corinne Gerson

THE
TWO-THOUSAND-POUND
GOLDFISH

by

Betsy Byars

AN
APPLE®
PAPERBACK

SCHOLASTIC INC.
New York Toronto London Auckland Sydney

ISBN 0-590-42368-1

12 11 10 9 8 7 6 5   1 2 3/9

Printed in the U.S.A.   28

For Charles Duffey

THE
TWO-THOUSAND-POUND
GOLDFISH

"If the cloud hits Los Angeles, it will reduce the entire population to the size of Barbie dolls within ten minutes!"

"Yes, Professor, unless . . ."

Warren sat in the second row of the theater, staring up at the screen. A piece of cold popcorn was in his hand, halfway to his mouth, forgotten.

—We've tried everything. Everything! Nothing can stop the monster.

—Wait! There's one thing we haven't tried.

—What?

—The S-F-342 Photo-Atomic cloud.

—But that's never been tested, Professor. There's no guarantee it will work.

—It's our one hope. Tell Doctor Barronni to ready the machine.

—But Professor—

"Warren Otis." The theater manager was coming down the aisle. "Is there a Warren Otis in the theater? Warren Otis!"

When his name was called for the third time, Warren straightened. "Oh, that's me. I'm Warren Otis. What do you want?"

"Your grandmother called. You're supposed to go home."

"Is something wrong?"

"She just said you're supposed to go home."

Warren got up out of his seat. Walking backward so he could watch the pink haze of the S-F-342 Photo-Atomic cloud encircle the monster, he moved slowly, reluctantly, up the aisle.

The monster inhaled some of the S-F-342 and began clawing at the sky. He threw back his head and roared. Drool came out of his mouth.

A poor effect, Warren decided, walking slower. You could see it was a man in a reptile suit now, standing in a pond made up to look like the Pacific Ocean. Economy drool, too—probably corn syrup.

—It's taking effect, Professor. The monster is shrinking.

—Wait! The wind is changing!

—Yes, Professor, the cloud is shifting. It's heading for Los Angeles!

Warren stopped. In the crook of his arm was his half-eaten box of popcorn. It had been there for six hours. Warren ate between features.

"Excuse me," a voice said.

"Sure." Warren shifted to let two girls pass. Eyes on the screen, he felt his way into an aisle seat in the last row.

—We've got to stop it!

—Professor! Look at the monster! It's still shrinking! The cloud works!

—Yes, this means—

—This means that if the cloud hits Los Angeles, it will reduce the entire population to the size of Barbie dolls within ten minutes!

—Yes, Professor, unless . . .

This was the third time Warren had heard that prediction this afternoon, but it was still awesome. His eyes gleamed. He envisioned millions of Barbies and Kens running helplessly around Los Angeles, trying to climb up into house-sized beds, making human ladders up to doorknobs, squeaking like mice as they scurried through the streets.

"Excuse me."

"Sure." A fat boy crawled over Warren's knees. He shifted impatiently to keep the screen in sight.

—There may be time enough if—

Warren's lips were moving with the actor's now, forming the words. "If," he and the actor said together, "we can send the cloud back out to—"

"Warren Otis!" It was the manager again. "Is Warren Otis still in the theater?"

Warren sighed aloud. He got up, head down, and ducked quickly into the lobby. He went around the refreshment center and out into the street, where he stood for a moment under the marquee.

He never came out of a theater without sensing all over again the cold drabness of the real world. The same dull line of traffic was in the street, the same dull sky overhead. Even the shadows seemed empty, nothing lurking inside.

Warren zipped up his jacket and pulled his aviator sunglasses down from on top of his head. Frowning slightly, he started down the sidewalk.

He felt as dissatisfied as if he had been interrupted in the middle of a dream. He began to eat his cold popcorn.

He stepped off the curb at the light and waited for it to change. He glanced down at his feet.

—What lives in the sewer beneath the city, weighs two thousand pounds, and is coming out tonight to get *you*?

That had been the advertisement for next Saturday's main feature. Warren looked down at the drain to see if he could catch the gleam of a two-thousand-pound alligator's eyes in the sewer below. All he saw were old candy wrappers and dead leaves.

The light changed, and Warren crossed the street slowly. Could there really be alligators under the city, he wondered, alligators bought by tourists in Florida years ago and then flushed down the toilet when they got big enough to snap at the family poodle?

It really could happen, he thought. His excitement rose. His sister had done that once with a goldfish—flushed it down the toilet.

Warren walked slower and then stopped in front of Walgreen's. Could his sister's goldfish— what was its name? Bubbles! Could Bubbles

[7]

still be down there? A two-thousand-pound gold-fish?

—What swims in the sewers below the city, weighs two thousand pounds, and wants to slurp you to death?

The movie would start with a picture of Bubbles. Her mouth would be opening and closing.

Warren broke off, frowning slightly. It was going to be hard to make Bubbles look scary, but with the right special effects man, anything was possible.

Warren's friend Eddie claimed he had once seen a horror movie about a giant tomato. A tomato! And all the tomato had done was roll around squashing people. And a girl in Warren's science class said she had seen a movie about giant, sixty-foot-tall rabbits that terrified the world, but Warren wasn't sure he believed that.

Tomatoes, bunny rabbits—it was pitiful. It was as bad as a horror movie about a cow, something Warren had once envisioned. At least his cow, Bossy, had gone around squirting radioactive milk on people, but still Warren had never been able to make the idea work. As soon as Bossy would lift her leg (and how else was she going to squirt milk?), well, as soon as she would lift her leg, some low-minded people in the audience would be sure to snicker. Warren didn't care much for comedy science fiction.

A woman bumped into Warren, and he mumbled, "Sorry," and started walking again.

It would be one of those goldfish with the big, bulging eyes, he decided, and because of some chemical in the sewer water—say a chemical company had been getting rid of dangerous waste material by illegally dumping it into the sewer—this dangerous waste material, say, XX-109, which had been developed to make beef cattle bigger, had turned the unsuspecting Bubbles into an enormous flesh-eating creature with a special craving for human beings. (See, that was why they had to stop giving XX-109 to the cattle. As an unpleasant side effect, they ate the cowboys.)

In the opening scene, before the credits, there would be two sewer workers having lunch in the depths of the sewer.

There would be dim lights, slapping of water against concrete, dripping pipes, oozing walls, scurrying of rats. Then silence.

[9]

"Things are quiet," one sewer worker would say while he unwrapped his hoagie.

"Yeah, too quiet," his co-worker would answer.

These were Warren's favorite lines. It had been impossible to work them into his cow horror movie because cows moo so often.

"Things are quiet."

"Yeah, too quiet."

"Moooooooooooooooooo."

It just wouldn't work. Here, it was perfect. Because as the co-worker said, "Yeah, too quiet," a ripple would appear in the dark waters below, the sliver of a golden fin would be seen curling ominously back and forth, swirling closer with each turn.

The two men would be so intent on their conversation they would not see the ripple or sense their approaching doom. "Hey, did you see Legs Madden on *Bowling for Dollars* last night?" one would be saying.

And Bubbles—Bubbles wouldn't have teeth, of course, but her mouth would have a sort of vacuum cleaner effect. She would *ingest* people. (Warren loved the word "ingest.") The only sign of warning would be one bubble.

In the deep ominous silence, it would come. BLOOOOP! And then a terrible churning of waters, flashes of gold, an enormous slurping sound, two fading screams, and then, again, silence. The camera would zoom in on the half-eaten hoagie at the water's edge.

Then the title would explode onto the screen. *GOLDFISH!*

Warren smiled to himself. And a close-up of the goldfish's mouth. A kind of pulsating sound would fill the theater, ominous, pounding . . . slurp . . . slurp . . . slurp . . . slurp. . . .

"Are you all right?" a woman asked, touching his arm. Warren started.

He realized he had been standing in the middle of the sidewalk, making goldfish mouths. "Oh yes, I'm fine." He swallowed. He felt he had to give an explanation for his strange behavior. "I was choking on a piece of popcorn."

"You should be more careful."

"I will."

The woman gave him one last look, shook her head, and moved on down the street.

Warren glanced around, startled to find that the street was dark, that the day had turned to night. He stuffed his popcorn box in a nearby trash can and crossed the street, running. Horns blew and drivers cursed as he zigzagged through the lines of cars.

"Same to you," he muttered beneath his breath.

"Snails! Millions of snails, man-eating snails. It's the slime of centuries!"

"I know. Don't slip."

Where have you been?" His grandmother stood in the hall, blocking Warren's way.

"I've been to the movies, Grandma. You know that." He glanced on either side of his grandmother to see if he could slip past. His grandmother seemed to have the ability to swell when she needed to. Now she filled the entire hallway.

"I'm not going through this every Saturday," she said.

"What?"

"Calling the theater and having you paged. Now you are either going to learn to come home on time or you are not going to the movies ever again. Do you understand me?"

"Yes!"

She shifted so that he could pass into the living room. "Your supper's on the table," she called after him. "It may be cold."

"*May* be," he muttered. He went into the kitchen. The faded baskets of food on the old wallpaper always reminded him of the food on the table—it was faded and tasteless too.

He sat down. His grandmother served everybody's plate at the same time, whether they were there or not. On the plate in front of him were cold, hardened mashed potatoes, limp beans, greasy Spam.

There was another plate beside his. The food on that one had not been eaten either.

"Where's Weezie?" he called.

"How would I know?" His grandmother was in the doorway now, watching him. "I am the last person to know where my grandchildren are. No one tells me anything!" She turned and went into her bedroom and slammed the door.

His grandmother loved to slam doors. It was

the only reason she had gone into the bedroom. Warren knew this. He knew too that she would wait just inside the door for a count of about thirty and then come out again.

He speared a bean on his fork. He was used to cold food, but his sister Weezie was usually on time. He felt a sudden chill of excitement.

Weezie was missing—Warren considered anyone who was five minutes late "missing." She had been on her way home from the library and . . . He lowered his fork, bean untouched. And on the way home from the library—what? She had fallen into the sewer?

How could Weezie fall into the sewer? They had grates over them, didn't they? And Weezie wasn't the type to pry up a grate.

Suddenly his head jerked up. A kitten! He smiled. Weezie was a pushover for stray kittens. She would hear a faint meow and look down into the grate— No, no, there would be a big pipe, an aqueduct that led into the sewer. And Weezie would walk in, her footsteps echoing hollowly down the walls. "Here, kitty, kitty, kitty."

Beyond her, in the dark water, there would appear a golden ripple, the flash of a swirling fin, the swish of deep, disturbed currents, the glint of an enormous eye, the whirl of primeval forces.

"Kitty, kitty, kitty."

Weezie would peer into the darkness. Then she would move slowly, deeper into the sewer. Weezie wasn't the kind to give up on a kitten.

"Kitty?"

A sudden stillness would fall in the sewer. Things are quiet around here, Weezie would think. In her mind a voice would answer, Too quiet.

But before she could heed the warning, it would come. BLOOOOOP! The warning bubble, and then the water would churn furiously, a golden form would rise up from the water, majestic and terrible, and then the awesome slurping noise, the fading scream of a young girl, and then, silence.

Warren sighed. He felt a pang of guilt. He always did when he allowed his relatives to be the victims in his horror movies. After he had allowed Bossy to squirt radioactive milk on Grandma, he had not slept well for two nights.

He got himself back to normal by reminding himself that he had warned her. "Don't go out, Grandma, please" had been his exact words. "The cow may squirt tonight."

"I'd like to see any cow squirt me!"

Well, she had.

Anyway, he would make up for letting Weezie be ingested by going out when his Grandma asked him to search for her. His grandma did that all the time. "Warren, go find Weezie" was a nightly order.

He heard his grandmother come out of her bedroom, and he waited, his face turned away. He opened his mouth at the same time she did, and he mouthed with her the words, "Warren, go find Weezie."

"Why do I always have to go find Weezie?" he asked. He turned, frowning. He was going to go, but it never hurt to put up a struggle.

"You want me to do it? Sixty years old and legs like balloons?"

"Why does anybody have to do it? Weezie can get home by herself. Nobody's going to mug her, if that's what you're afraid of. Weezie's big. Muggers only go after weak, pitiful targets—like me."

"Go."

"Well, I haven't finished eating yet."

"So eat."

"That's what I'm trying to do." He put the cold bean in his mouth.

"Now go."

"One bean is eating? Oh, all right!" He got up slowly, as if he were as old as his grandmother. "Why don't you just call the library?" he asked. "You know that's where she is."

She watched him without speaking.

"That's what you'd do to me. 'Is Warren Otis in the theater? Warren Otis, go home.' How do you think that makes me feel?"

"It should make you want to be home on time."

"Well, it doesn't."

"And when you find her, you two come straight home."

He left the apartment, slipped down the stairs and out into the night. He zipped his jacket up against the cold.

Now that he was outside, he walked slower. The only person who had never been a victim in one of his horror movies was his mother. Even he, himself, had been carried off by rabid bats.

And in *The Revenge of the Snails,* a budget horror movie he had created for television, he had narrowly missed being slimed to death, which had to be one of the least pleasant ways to die he could imagine.

He and his friend Eddie had gone to the old fishing hole and had been drawn by curiosity to the odd crust on top and the slime around the sides. They had stepped closer.

"Snails! Millions of snails, man-eating snails," he had said. "It's the slime of centuries."

"I know. Don't slip."

At that very moment Warren's foot had slid out from under him. "Aaaaaaa—" He had fallen into the pond. If he hadn't been quick-witted, if he hadn't scrambled up as soon as he heard the dreaded crunch of shells, if Eddie hadn't extended a hand and pulled him up, well, then he would have been done for.

But his mother—nothing bad happened to her. He wouldn't let it. Maybe that was because, of them all, his mother was the most likely to have something happen to her in real life. She had enough danger without radioactive cows and man-eating snails.

He rounded the corner. The library was just ahead. Warren slowed down. He was planning to enter the sewer himself and discover that Weezie was missing. Her books would be there, her name written carefully inside them, and he would—

Suddenly Warren stopped. He saw that Weezie was in the phone booth in front of the library. She was talking to somebody on the phone. Warren moved closer.

He was curious. Weezie was not the type to talk on the phone unless there was a reason. Suddenly he wanted to know what that reason was. It might be something secret, and he could hold it over her, make her do things for him. Keeping close to the buildings, out of the streetlight, he moved toward the phone booth.

As he got closer he saw that Weezie was listening, not talking. She was so intent, he felt she would not have noticed him even if he had rapped on the glass door.

He went closer. There were tears on Weezie's cheeks. He was stunned. He had never known Weezie to cry, had never been aware she could cry. It was like learning that Muhammad Ali cries.

He stood in the shadows, staring in awe at his sister. She hung up the phone and waited with her head bowed. To Warren it was like the moment in a horror movie when the werewolf has changed back into human form and needs a moment to compose himself before going back to the world.

Weezie lifted her head, opened the door to the

booth, and stepped out into the night air.

"Who were you talking to?" Warren asked abruptly, counting on surprise to get an answer.

Weezie spun around. She crossed the sidewalk in three steps. "What are you doing here?" She grabbed him by the upper arm.

"Ow! Let go! Grandma sent me!"

She stared at him and then abruptly let him free. He moved back a step, out of reach. He rubbed his arm. "Who were you talking to?"

"Nobody."

"Is that why you were *crying*?" he went on, sneering slightly. "Because it was nobody?"

"I was not crying."

"Your cheeks are still wet."

"I was not crying!" She towered over him now, as menacing as anything he had ever created in his movies.

"You were!"

"And if you mention to Grandma, just mention, that I was on the phone . . ." She trailed off, leaving the threat hanging.

"If I mention it to Grandma, then what?"

"I promise you will be sorry."

She turned and started for home. He watched her, her high, straight back, her long legs. There was something so imposing in her walk—it reminded him of John Wayne—Warren decided not to say anything.

"I'll tell if I want to!" he yelled defiantly.

She did not turn around, and after a moment he began to follow, the two-thousand-pound goldfish forgotten for the moment.

"There's something down there. I don't know what, and I don't know why. But there is something down there."

"And heaven help us if it ever decides to come up."

Warren lay in bed, watching the reflection of car lights on the ceiling. He could not sleep. He could not get Weezie's phone call out of his mind. He wanted to know who had made Weezie cry. It was no mere boyfriend, no girl friend. He was sure of that. It was no clerk at a store, no operator, no—

And then it came to him. Weezie had been talking to their mother!

He sat up in bed, mouth open, staring ahead without seeing. He didn't know how it could be possible—everything told him it couldn't be—and yet he knew, *knew* that's who it had been.

He leaned forward over his knees. He felt as if his entire body had been thrown into a higher gear, that his thoughts, his blood, everything was moving faster. His mother!

For the past three years Warren had seen his mother only on the evening news and in newspaper pictures. The postcards she sent them were mailed from places where she had never been. This was in case the FBI was watching the mail. Warren's mother lived in a fugitive world that Warren only half understood.

Warren's actual memory of his mother—drawn from the first five years of his life—was that of a woman always on the move, a woman with a sort of frantic urgency in her voice and movements. She carried signs protesting the Vietnam War in front of the White House. She lay down in front of nuclear power plants that polluted the environment. She was carried kicking and struggling to a patrol car to call attention to the dangers of pesticides.

His mother took on the glow, the mystery, of Wonder Woman, a person bigger than life, strong enough to make the world right. He saw her as being like Atlas, with the entire world on her shoulders.

When he was five, everything changed. Warren's mother became part of a movement that was no longer peaceful. She went from putting stink bombs in the ventilating system of the Hilton, where a nuclear energy conference was being held, to pipe bombs exploded at night in chemical plants, Molotov cocktails thrown at executive limousines. And Warren's mother became wanted by the FBI, and she could never come home again.

Warren could no longer picture his mother in his mind. She had used so many names, worn so many disguises. Sometimes in newspaper pictures her hair was black, sometimes blond. Sometimes she wore white-rimmed Woolworth's sunglasses, sometimes wire spectacles. Sometimes she was old, sometimes young. He was painfully aware that he would no longer recognize his mother if he passed her on the street.

"Your mother is dead," his grandmother would say flatly. She would not even allow her name to be mentioned in the apartment. "I only have two daughters now."

"You have three!" he used to protest. "Ginger and Pepper *and* Saffron!"

Grandma had named her three daughters for spices. Aunt Pepper had told him that when Grandma used to call them from the window, she sounded like an old spice peddler. "Ginger! Pepper! Saffron!"

Warren's mom, Saffron, was the only one who had a nickname—Saffee, to him the most beautiful name in the world.

And now Weezie had talked to her on the telephone! He was sure of that. He wanted to rush into her room and shake her awake. "You talked to Mom!"

The impulse was so strong that he actually got up out of bed, against his will, like a sleepwalker. He took a few steps toward the door. He stopped.

He knew how Weezie would react. She would be furious, and as usual her anger would be turned to scorn. Scorn was her best weapon. "Talking to Mom!" she would say, her voice adult and terrible. "Do you still hang on to the precious little dream that Mommie will come home, pick you up, kiss you, and make it all better?"

He moved back and sat on the edge of his bed like someone who had taken a blow. He *had* hung on to that dream for a long time. He had hurried home from school again and again because he had a "feeling" that she would be there, had run up the steps with so much momentum that if she had been there to pick him up, they would have spun around like skaters.

He lay down on the bed and pulled the covers over his shivering body. He stared up at the ceiling. He was as hurt as if his sister had actually said the words to him.

He closed his eyes and tried to get back into the mood of the sewer. He imagined himself walking beneath the dripping walls, shivering, his footsteps echoing hollowly down the long tunnels. He imagined that warning BLOOP, imagined swirling around as the golden form, majestic and terrible, rose from the dark waters, imagined his scream. "AAAAAAAAAAAAAaaaaaaaaaaa. . . ."

Of course, not wishing to do away with himself so early in the film, he would somehow have to prevent Bubbles from actually ingesting him. Perhaps . . . His thoughts died from lack of interest.

Usually his movies took him out of his world instantly. Sometimes a single sentence, spoken in a low tone: "No ordinary creature ate this whole herd of cattle." Well, something like that, and he would be off.

Tonight, nothing would work. Only an hour earlier the sewer had been the realest thing in the world. The sights, smells, and sounds had filled his mind completely. Now the sewer was as foreign as something out of a history lesson.

All of a sudden Warren wanted his mom. And he wanted her in the old dreamlike way. He wanted to be scooped up in her thin arms, spun around, kissed. That was the only thing in the world that could take away this terrible feeling of loneliness.

He threw back his limp covers and kicked them away. He walked slowly into the hall.

He paused to listen. His grandmother was snoring in the living room. She had fallen asleep watching an Elvis Presley movie, and now there was nothing but snow on the screen. In the morning she would complain about missing the end.

He went into Weezie's room and stumbled over her shoes in the dark.

"Who's there?" she asked, sitting quickly up in bed.

"It's just me."

"What are you doing in here? Are you sick?"

"No."

"Is Grandma all right?"

"I guess so. She's snoring."

"Then go back to bed. You know I don't like people in my room."

He stood a few feet away from her, on the latch-hooked rug his grandmother had made from a kit.

"Go on, Warren."

Warren did not move. He usually avoided the bare floor. When he was little and home alone he would circle the entire apartment, leaping from chair to sofa, crawling over end tables, onto the TV set, over kitchen counters, the stove, anything to keep from stepping on the floor. It was a game he played. All his games back then were escape games, even when the bare floor was all he had to escape. Now, out of habit, he waited on the rug.

"Are you still there?" Weezie asked, her voice rising with irritation. "I do not like people watching me sleep!"

"You weren't drooling."

"Warren, get out of here. I mean it now." She groped on the floor for something to throw at him.

There was a pause. Warren curled his toes down into the soft wool of his grandmother's rug for strength, a plant taking root. "Were you talking to Mom on the telephone tonight?"

"Mom? Is that what you woke me up for? *Mom?* Don't be ridiculous. Go back to bed."

She turned over, pulling the covers around her, and sighed. He continued to watch his sister. He knew she was not asleep.

He shifted, rubbed one foot over the other. *"Were* you talking to Mom?"

As Warren stood there, waiting for an answer, he felt as if he had spent most of his life pleading with women, waiting for answers. Usually, though, with Weezie, he just had to beg her to listen to his movies.

"Want to hear a movie I'm planning?"

"In a word—no."

"Please, Weezie, you'll like this one. Please. It starts out with an explosion in the desert and some scientists come to investigate and they look down inside this enormous crack in the surface of the earth and they see something stirring. One of the scientists says, 'There's something down there. I don't know what, and I don't know why, but there is something down there.' And the other one answers, 'And heaven help us if it ever decides to come up.' "

He hated to plead with people. It made him feel smaller somehow. He watched Weezie's back. He cleared his throat and said again, "*Was* it Mom?"

Suddenly Weezie came up out of the covers like a tornado. She whirled to face him, throwing back the sheet. Her hands fell on her hips as naturally as tree limbs spring back into place.

"All right, just try to be sensible for once in your life," she snapped. "How do you think I could be talking to Mom?" Her voice was more scornful than Warren had feared.

"I don't know . . . exactly."

"The last time we heard from her was four months ago, do you realize that? A postcard from California. 'Having a wonderful time, glad you aren't here.' "

"That was the last time *I* heard from her," he said pointedly.

"So, do you think I have some secret line of communication? What? You think I send out pigeons? Smoke signals? Wireless messages? Voodoo drums? Call me tonight at sevennnnn." Her hands fluttered mysteriously to make it all seem more impossible.

"I think . . . somehow . . . the telephone."

Weezie exhaled with disgust. "Oh, go to bed, Warren." She fell back onto her pillow to show that the conversation was over.

Warren waited in silence. In his movies, discoveries came so easily. "These scorpions are from the Incan cave." "This woman was squirted by radioactive milk with two percent butterfat." It was only in real life that you couldn't get answers. "I'm not going, Weezie, until you tell me who you were talking to."

"All right. I was talking to a girl from school."

"I don't believe you. A girl from school made you cry? Come on. I've seen the girls at your school, and there's not one who—"

"All right, a boy from my school."

"I don't believe that either."

"He was going to take me to the prom, and now he's going to take Isolee Watkins." She looked at him through her lashes. Then she raised her head. "Satisfied?"

"No."

"Well, it's all you're going to get."

The way she looked at him then, with her eyes as hard as stone, her mouth set, told Warren it was hopeless. He had seen that look before.

He turned and walked to his room, past the living room where the blank TV crackled. As he lay down and turned his face to the wall, his mouth was as set as hers.

"No, no, it can't be. No goldfish can weigh two thousand pounds. Why, a goldfish that big could ingest . . ."

"Go ahead and finish, Chief. Could ingest two sewer workers."

"Get up if you're going to Pepper's," his grandmother called from the doorway.

"What?"

"Get up."

Warren lay blinking in the sunlight from the window. All night he had suffered through one dream after another. He was never lucky enough to have good scary dreams with monsters and space creatures.

In his dreams he searched for lost homework, was sent to a blackboard too tall to reach, worked with pencils that squealed and caused students to laugh, and wrote on paper that spread across his desk like milk. Now he lay on his dirty sheets, more tired than if he had not slept at all.

"Is Weezie going?" he called.

"To Pepper's? No."

"Then I'm not going either."

"Well, then you'll be here all day by yourself."

He rose on one elbow, alert at last. "Why? Where's Weezie?"

"She went out. Now come on, get dressed. We'll miss the bus."

"Where did Weezie go?"

"I don't know. To the library."

"The library's not open on Sunday morning."

"Well, I don't know. She said she was going to study with somebody. Maria maybe. Or Isolee."

In one move he was on the floor, looking out the window at the street below.

The sidewalks were empty except for two dogs lying in front of the corner grocery store. These two dogs made up the neighborhood pack. The dog warden had been trying to catch them for years, but they were too smart for him. They knew the crawl spaces under every house, the broken slats in every fence. Now, sensing it was

Sunday, the warden's day off, they lay openly soaking up the morning sun.

"Why didn't you tell me Weezie was going out?" He struck the windowsill with his fists.

"Why all this sudden interest in Weezie's goings and comings?"

"Nothing. I just like to know what she's doing."

"She's studying."

"She *says* she's studying."

He turned away from the sunny window and looked at his grandmother. She watched him for a moment and then shrugged. "Weezie's generally doing what she says she's doing."

"A lot you know."

Her eyes narrowed. "Are you trying to tell me something about your sister?"

He sighed. "No."

"Then get dressed and let's go."

Warren stood on the dusty floor. His grandmother thought it was a waste of energy to sweep floors more than once a month. He pulled on his clothes, the same he had worn yesterday. His grandmother didn't believe in washing clothes often either.

Then he continued to stand in the middle of the

floor, his teeth clamped tightly together, wondering where his sister was, what she was doing. He had the feeling she was contacting his mother, phoning her, maybe even going to see her. He struck an imaginary windowsill.

"You ready?"

"Yes."

He went out of the apartment and down the stairs behind his grandmother. She took the steps slowly, one by one, like a child.

Warren paused on the landing. He put on his aviator sunglasses, hiding the fury in his eyes. Never before, in all the years of his mother's absence—years in which he had missed her and longed for her and wept more tears for her than anybody—never in all those years had he even considered the possibility of finding her. If he had thought it was possible he would have been roaming the earth like a nomad.

And now Weezie had—

"Come on. I hear the bus," his grandmother called up, holding the door open. "It's coming."

He ran down the rest of the steps and out onto the sidewalk. His grandmother was at the curb, ready to board.

And now, he thought, Weezie had done that.

She had somehow found their mother, had talked to her, maybe at this very moment was on her way to see her.

"How's it going?" his grandmother asked the driver as she climbed up. She always sat behind the driver, ignoring the signs, and spent the time chatting. "My daughter Pepper's having us to dinner. You know Pepper?" she asked as she settled herself in the side seat.

"No'm."

"She rides this bus—a tall girl, light red hair?"

"Lots of redheads on this route."

"I thought you might remember her because when she was living in New York she had a part in a soap opera."

"My wife might. She watches all them shows."

"I remember when Pepper got the part. I sat back and thought, Well, now I'll have the pleasure of watching my daughter every afternoon. She'll get married and divorced and go crazy and attempt suicide. Only guess what?"

The driver shook his head.

"She was on seven episodes and got killed in a car crash. Burned up. They never found the body."

"My, my."

"For a while I hoped she didn't really get killed, just thrown clear of the wreck and was wandering around somewhere with amnesia. Only it's been three years now, so I guess it won't happen."

"Don't look like it."

"I have two daughters." She glanced sideways at Warren. "The other daughter's a singer in— Oh, here's our stop." She got up and Warren followed. She went down the steps slowly. "I got bad legs," she explained to the driver.

"Take your time," he answered.

They walked the block to Pepper's apartment while his grandmother talked about bus drivers. She liked them. No bus driver had ever—in her fifty years of riding buses—been rude to her.

She shuffled along the sidewalk. She wore her best bedroom slippers. "And I'm not the ideal fare," she admitted. "I don't get on fast. Half the time I don't have the right change. I—" She paused to ring the bell to Pepper's apartment.

"Come on in," Pepper called. "I'm cooking."

"That's encouraging. Usually she's defrosting."

"Grandma!"

Grandma felt her way to the sofa and put her

swollen legs up on the coffee table. "You two socialize," she said. "I'll rest."

Warren went into the kitchen where Aunt Pepper was reading the instructions on a package of frozen lasagna. "Sit down," she said with a grin, "and tell me about your latest movie." Aunt Pepper was the only person who was really interested in his plots. "I hope there's a good part for me."

"It's about a goldfish," he said without his usual enthusiasm.

"What is this? Some sort of a nature study?"

"No, it's a two-thousand-pound goldfish. See, it got flushed into the sewer and has grown to enormous size because of a chemical in the water."

"I like that."

"You like them all."

"No, no, I did not like *The Revenge of the Snails*. I refused to be slimed to death, remember? I have my principles. Anyway, what does this goldfish do, swallow people?"

"Ingests them."

"Ah, and somebody says, 'No, no, it can't be. No goldfish can weigh two thousand pounds. Why, a goldfish that big could ingest . . .' 'Go ahead and finish, Chief. Could ingest . . .'" She paused and looked at Warren, waiting.

"Two sewer workers," he supplied.

"This goldfish has ingested two sewer workers? I love it. Can I have a part in the movie?"

He nodded.

"How about this. I come into the sewer. I am pursued by a mugger and I hide behind a pipe. The mugger spots me and starts for me. Suddenly he sees a look of horror come over my face. He thinks, naturally, that I am horrified because of him, but actually it is because I see an enormous, giant goldfish rising out of the water behind him. I scream, 'Look out behind you!' He says, 'Lady, that is the oldest trick in the book,' and at that moment—" Pepper broke off. "What's wrong? Aren't you interested? I was just getting into my role."

"Nothing's wrong," he said.

"You can tell me."

"It's nothing!"

Aunt Pepper waited. She knew that when Warren claimed nothing was wrong, he usually broke down on his own and told what the trouble was. "Well." He looked up at his aunt. "What's wrong is that I think Weezie knows where Mom is."

"Did she tell you that?"

"Weezie talked to Mom on the phone."

"Did she tell you *that?*"

"No, but I know it's true. Everybody probably knows where Mom is but me."

"I don't know where your mom is, and I don't think Weezie does either." She sat down at the table across from Warren. She glanced at the door to the living room and lowered her voice.

"All right, you might as well know this. Once a month—on the first Monday at seven o'clock—your mom calls the phone booth in front of the library. Or that's when she's supposed to call. One of us, Weezie or me, goes there and waits. Sometimes she calls and sometimes she doesn't. It's her way of keeping in touch."

He sat up straighter. "How long has this been going on?"

"In the past three years your mom has called maybe six or seven times. She asks about you and Grandma and Weezie, and that's it. We never talk about where she is or what she's doing."

"I want to talk to her."

"Honey, your mom has broken the law."

"I know that, but—"

"Once you've broken the law, it stays broken. It's like smashing that glass right there. And afterward you can be sorry for what you did, and you

[42]

can live like a saint, but that doesn't wipe out what you did."

"I *know* that!"

"Look at Abbie Hoffman. He's been living in some town in New York, a model citizen. He served on local committees. A governor commended him for some special service. But none of that wiped out the fact that he broke the law."

"I don't want to hear about him."

"I'm telling you so you can understand why your mom can't come home and be a mom and why you can't call her and visit her. Your mom has broken the law, and she's got two choices. She can live in hiding, or she can go to prison."

"That doesn't mean I can't talk to her like you do. Maybe if I talked to her, I could go see her. Maybe I could—"

There was a noise in the doorway. Warren looked up to see his grandmother.

"Mom, we're talking about Saffee," Pepper said in a gentle voice.

"I don't know any Saffee," his grandmother answered and, turning away, went back and sat heavily on the old sofa.

"It's got to be destroyed. We can't have a two-thousand-pound fish swimming under our city."

"I agree. Our sewer must be made safe for mankind."

Warren was standing at the window, watching for his sister to return. His grandmother was in the living room in front of the television set. Usually his grandmother turned on the TV first thing, the way other people switch on lights, but tonight the house was dark and silent.

Warren's thoughts turned from the dreary, empty street to the sewer below it. There Bubbles waited in the dark swirling waters.

Warren had always had strong feelings for his individual monsters. The creatures who attacked in groups—the snails and the cockroaches and the leeches—he could never work up much sentiment about them. But the individuals—Bossy, the giant skunk—he cared about them.

Even so, Warren believed he had a special feeling for Bubbles. Perhaps it was because Bubbles was one of those saddest of creatures who are peaceful by nature and who are, because of man's careless stupidity, turned into something that has to be destroyed.

He knew he was going to hate it when that happened to Bubbles. *If*, that is, he ever destroyed Bubbles.

Oh, sooner or later someone would get around to saying, "It's got to be destroyed. We can't have a two-thousand-pound fish swimming under our city." And someone else would answer, "I agree. Our sewer must be made safe for mankind."

But at the moment nothing was happening. Bubbles was swimming freely through the waters of the sewer, stirring the long, green slime on the walls, causing eddies in the dark water.

It was the point in a movie where the director would have to build up suspense with a few cutbacks to dangerous pictures of Bubbles' mouth. Slurp . . . slurp . . . slurp. . . .

Warren straightened. Maybe the two neighborhood dogs could come into the sewer for shelter from the dog warden, and Bubbles could ingest them. Warren imagined the two dogs, dusty, tired, glancing over their shoulders, lumbering into the sewer, falling down on the hard cement like two bags of bones.

Warren discarded the idea. He never let anything happen to mongrel dogs unless he absolutely had to. And he liked the neighborhood dog pack. He was proud of the way they escaped the law.

Perhaps a policeman on horseback could come into the sewer. The horse would sense something was wrong and be skittish, but the policeman would . . .

Warren became so engrossed in the thought that he did not see Weezie come around the corner of the drugstore. Then, for a moment, he didn't recognize her because she was bent forward like a person struggling against a strong wind.

When Warren saw it was Weezie, he leaned forward so abruptly he struck his head on the window. He turned and started for the door.

"What is it?" his grandmother said, sitting up

straight, startled out of a dream. "Has something happened?"

"No."

Warren went out the door and down the stairs so quickly he met Weezie out on the sidewalk. "Where have you been all day?"

"Don't bother me."

Weezie looked even older, more tired. She never wore makeup, and now she looked like she needed some. She attempted to push past Warren, but, for once, he was the stronger.

"Where have you been?"

Weezie rested one hand on her hip in an old gesture of defiance that now only made her look more tired. "I would like to go upstairs," she said.

Warren was blocking the doorway, filling it like his grandmother. "Have you seen Mom?"

"Warren," she said, "did it ever occur to you that seeing Mom might not be the wonderful, glorious event you think it's going to be?"

"No!" He paused, then said, "What do you mean?"

"I mean that you think finding Mom would be the greatest thing that has ever happened in the world. It would be like old times—"

"It would!"

"Only it would have to be better than old times to be all right, because you do remember what the old times were like, don't you?"

There was a hard note to Weezie's voice. Warren shifted uneasily, squinting at her, though there was no glare from the late-afternoon sun.

"The old times, the good old days you want to recreate, were Mom rushing in and out of the house and you and me trying desperately to get her attention and tell her something that had happened at school or something we were worried about and her saying, 'Go on, go on, I'm listening,' while she painted signs and cut out pictures of injured Vietnamese and made telephone calls. That was all we ever were to Mom—a background noise, like the radio, something to listen to while she was busy with what really interested her. The only reason she had us was because she was anti-abortion."

"That's not true."

"Do you realize it has been three years since we even saw her?"

"I can count."

"And because it's been so long, it's easy to deceive yourself, don't you understand that? It's easy to believe that—oh, if Mom would only

[48]

come home everything would be all right—"

"It would!"

"All right, let's be realistic, Warren. Suppose we found Mom. Suppose we performed a superhuman feat and found her. Do you honestly believe that she would welcome us with open arms?"

"Yes!"

"Or do you believe that she wouldn't be interested in us at all, that we would just be leftovers from a life she's left behind?"

"It wouldn't be like that. She can't be with us because of the police. It's the police that—"

"You know what it's like to me? It's like a long time ago when girls used to have babies when they weren't married. Back then the girls would go away and have their babies and give them up for adoption and then pretend it never happened. The next-door neighbors wouldn't even know about it."

He looked at her, puzzled. "That didn't happen to us. She didn't put us up for adoption."

"Let me finish. Today you hear a lot of stories about those adopted kids trying to find their real mothers, only—here's the point—the real mothers don't want to be found."

"Our mom is not like that."

She looked at him, her brown eyes serious. "That's the way it seems to me." She made a move to pass him, and he, silenced for the moment, did not try to stop her.

He watched Weezie go up the stairs. She was pulling herself along by the banister. "Anyway," he called, his defiance returning, 'Pepper told me that Mom calls every month. If she calls every month she must care about us."

"Five calls in three years," Weezie said without turning around.

"I thought it was more than that. Pepper said six or seven."

"Five calls."

"Still, she called!"

Suddenly Warren was overcome with the wish that he had a mother who didn't care so much about the world. He wished she had never even thought about future generations or atrocities in Asia. He wanted a mother who had smaller concerns. He wanted one of those mothers he saw in Sky City, standing in line to have their children's pictures made, the children as clean and combed as if they'd just come out of a box.

He leaned against the doorway. He was breathing with effort, as if he'd been running.

He wanted a mother who cared what he got on his report card and came to school for conferences and raised a fuss when his pictures weren't up on the bulletin board. He wanted a mother who would make cupcakes for the Halloween carnival and make him go to Sunday School on Sunday and—

Suddenly he straightened. He began to run up the stairs after Weezie. He slipped, went down on one knee, and scrambled to his feet.

Weezie was waiting for him on the second landing, looking down at him with a kind of sadness. Before he could ask his question she said, "No, I did not see our mother, but I can tell you for a fact that you are not going to like finding her."

"What?"

"You're not going to like what you find."

All of a sudden Weezie no longer looked like his sister. She was a stranger. He put one hand on the banister to steady himself.

Weezie waited, watching him with her dark eyes. Warren and Weezie had different fathers. Weezie's father lived in the city and gave money for her support and was learning computer science. Warren's father lived a fugitive life like his mother and sent no money. Warren felt it was that difference that was important now. Weezie actually looked like her father now. He probably looked like his.

Weezie opened the door and went into the apartment. Warren did not move.

There had been something in Weezie's manner, something serious and deep, that had made him stop. This warning—if that's what it had been—left him with such a strong feeling of dread that he had no desire to run after her with more questions.

He had the feeling, new and strange to him, that whatever Weezie knew was unhappy information, something that could wait, like a report card. He ran his tongue over his dry lips.

"Excuse me, Warren." It was Mrs. Oglesby, coming down the steps. He moved dutifully to the wall. "There's a good boy." She patted his head as if he were a puppy.

He waited, leaning against the wall. Then slowly, feeling tired himself, he began to climb the rest of the stairs.

"Chief, the monster appears to go for old women."

"*Mean* old women, from the looks of this one."

Warren was reading the old postcards from his mother. It was night, the light was poor, and he was in the bathroom, sitting on the side of the tub, reading from the streetlight. The poor light didn't matter. Warren knew the words by heart.

Dears—

His mom's handwriting had a rushed, spidery look. He could barely make out the words in good light.

Dears—Things have been going well—great progress on the media front. Did you see the news coverage of the White House protest last month? I was there—plaid coat, big green hat (borrowed finery as usual). Hope you saw me. I didn't chain myself to the fence so that (if necessary) I could flyyyyyyy. Be good. Remember me.

Miss you. Saff.

The postcards were dark with fingerprints, limp from many readings. They were post-office cards—no pictures of palm trees or mountains or monuments to linger over.

Dears—

That was the way she always started. He wished just once she would use his name. Dear *Warren* would mean a lot to him.

Dears—Today we went swimming and ate hot dogs and did the things we will all do together when the world is *right.* I thought of you because on one of the rides—we were at an amusement park (business *with* pleasure; we glued 2,000 "No Nukes" bumper stickers on cars)—anyway, on one of the rides were a boy and girl who reminded me of you—

By now she was at the bottom of the card, and the handwriting was smaller, the letters cramped.

[54]

The personal messages, the parts Warren cherished, were always written like this. He had to have Weezie make them out.

—laughing and happy, and that's the way I hope you two are. Love me. Miss me. Saff.

He shifted uncomfortably. The edge of the tub was hard, and his seat bones needed more flesh. Still, he kept sitting there, turning through the postcards, trying to find some proof that what his sister had implied was not true.

He knew that his mother loved him and missed him and wanted him with her. He knew it! Yet the almost careless freedom of the postcard messages . . . The postcards came from everywhere, it seemed, places he wouldn't have minded visiting himself—the amusement park, the White House.

This flitting around made her seem more like a creature of nature than a mother. She was like a bird or a moth. And—

He bent over the cards, searching each one in turn. His eyes were hard and narrow, a scientist looking for evidence.

And it did not really seem like she was saving the world. Marches and bumper stickers didn't seem like a Wonder Woman struggle. He felt a faint stirring of guilt as this unsettling thought took root and grew.

He began going through the cards slower, carefully turning through the limp pieces of paper. Nowhere—not on any postcard—could he find a mention of hardship, of loneliness. Sure, right here she said, "Love you. Miss you," but she hadn't even bothered to make those thoughts into complete sentences.

And lots of times it was "Love me. Remember me. Miss me."

He paused, frowning slightly, and read again the message about the amusement park. When he had first received this card, he had loved hearing about the bumper stickers. He remembered he had stood in the hall smiling, as he imagined his mother creeping through the parking lot, her red head bowed, applying the bumper stickers to Cadillacs and Jeeps alike.

Now there was no pleasure in it. He felt betrayed.

He thought back to the last time he had seen his mother. She had come into his room one night in her nightgown, clean, her long, curly hair smelling of soap. "Are you asleep, Warren?"

[56]

"No, no." He had been awake instantly. He had struggled into a sitting position.

"How's my pumpkin?" She had hugged him. Her thin body always felt a few degrees cooler than everybody else's.

"I'm fine. How long are you going to be here?" This was always his first question.

"Just tonight. Tomorrow we're on the march." Smiling, she held up one fist in a pretense of defiance.

He did not smile back. His face began to crumple. "Why don't you stay?"

"I can't, hon."

"Why?"

"Oh, pumpkin, the government's just like a great, terrible ball, and when it starts rolling it crushes half of what it rolls over and picks up the other half. And it gets bigger and bigger and more powerful, and somebody's got to stop it."

"Not you."

"I've got to try."

"I don't want you to go."

"I don't want to go either. I'm not even supposed to be here. I am risking arrest to sleep in my own bed and wash my hair in my own basin and kiss my own children good night."

"Then don't go."

"I have to."

After she left the room, Warren crawled out of bed and listened as his mom and Aunt Pepper talked in the living room. He could hear only parts of the conversation—his mother was talking in a low excited voice—but he got the picture of things done at night, a kind of adult Halloween.

There had been a raid on a nuclear plant. In his mind he could see his mother, face blackened, dark clothes, driving along in an old car at night, explosives in the trunk. He saw her slipping under barbed wire, over barricades, setting explosives while someone else, miles away, waiting in a phone booth, called in the bomb threat.

"I have never hurt anybody," she was telling Pepper.

"Not even your kids?" Aunt Pepper asked.

Warren glanced around the doorway then, startled at the question, and his mother's face, scrubbed so clean it shone in the lamplight, was like it contained a light of its own.

"The kids understand," she answered.

Warren had gone back to bed then, bent over because his stomach had started to hurt, yet knowing that his mother had to do these things. She was

Joan of Arc. She alone could save the troubled world.

But now . . . He glanced down at the postcards.

"Dears— Today's my birthday, so I decided to give myself a present. I went out and—"

The bathroom door opened suddenly, and Warren's head snapped up. There was his grandmother in the doorway. She turned on the light and started at the sight of him on the edge of the tub.

"What are you doing in here?" she asked.

"Nothing." Blinking in the bright light, he palmed the postcards like a magician and held them flat against his thigh, out of sight. He got quickly to his feet. "I better get to bed. School tomorrow."

"What's that you're hiding?"

"I'm not hiding anything. What?" He glanced around innocently, holding out his free hand. "Where?"

"There!"

With surprising strength she jerked up his arm, and the postcards from his mother clattered to the floor like old playing cards. His grandmother sighed. She knew what they were without looking down.

She stared at Warren. The look in her eyes acknowledged his childish stupidity.

Suddenly he felt a rush of anger. "Don't look at me like that!"

Her look did not change. She rested one hip against the basin and crossed her arms over her faded bathrobe, settling in for a long siege.

"I said, don't look at me like that!"

He rushed across the cracked linoleum, his hands raised, clenched into fists. He was ready to strike her. "My mother is alive and she cares about me and she wants me and she'll come get me when she can!"

Her look did not change.

His fists, raised on either side of his face, trembled, threatening to strike. He breathed in through his teeth. "You better not look at me like that!"

"Well, if you don't like the way I look, go ahead and hit me," she said, her old voice surprisingly steady. "If this is what my life's come to, you just go ahead and hit me."

"I will!"

"If this is what my whole life boils down to—one daughter in Las Vegas I haven't seen in two years, one who's a wanted criminal, a granddaughter that thinks she's too smart for me, and a grandson who waits in the bathroom in the middle of the night to strike me—well, if that's what life is, just go ahead and strike!"

Warren lowered his hands, rubbing his fingers uneasily over his thumbs. "I wasn't waiting in here to hit you, you know that."

"I've worked all my life. I've raised my children and looked after my family and this is what it's come to—being attacked by my own grandson."

"I'm not attacking you." He stepped back. "You just took me by surprise. Look, don't get upset." It scared him when his grandmother got like this, agitated and resentful, winding herself up so tightly she would be awake all night, roaming the house, pressing her hands against her heart.

Suddenly she sighed. "Oh, go to bed," she said in a flat, tired voice. Warren nodded gratefully, glad to be dismissed.

He stepped back and bent to pick up the postcards. In a sudden move his grandmother reached out and stepped on them, covering them firmly with her felt bedroom slipper.

"Grandma!" He attempted to free one of the cards and tore off the corner. "Grandma!" He was truly distressed now. "These are postcards from Mom!" It was as if she were defiling something sacred. "Grandma!"

She did not answer. Warren tugged at her ankle. "Let go!" But her leg was planted as firmly as a tree. "Let go!" There was more power in those doughlike ankles than he had thought.

"Grandma!" He glanced up to see if she was playing some sort of painful, teasing game, to see if she was going to lift her foot on her own and say, "Take your cards, but the next time I find you in here . . ."

It was no game. His grandmother was looking at him with eyes like steel. Her wrinkled face was set. "Go to bed," she said.

He looked at her for a moment, and then he got up slowly, accepting defeat. At the door he glanced back at his grandmother. Her head was raised, her chin high, her eyes stared so hard at the discolored tile that Warren felt her look went all the way through the wall to the street beyond.

"Anyway," he said as he stumbled down the hall to his room, "I know them by heart."

He flopped onto his bed. He closed his eyes. In his next movie, he decided, his grandmother would be the first victim.

"The monster, Chief, appears to go for old women," the policeman who discovered her body would say.

"*Mean* old women, from the looks of this one."

Exactly.

> "Do you smell what I smell?"
> "It smells like . . ."
> "Exactly what I was thinking."

At last something was happening in his goldfish movie. He could always count on something happening in his movies during first period—Language Arts. Once, he had completed an entire and complicated movie about an enormous skunk that terrorized the residents of an isolated western community.

Skunk! had been the title (although he had originally considered *Phew!*), and in *Skunk!*, one by one, the people tried to ride out of the endangered town and get badly needed help. It was like one of those westerns where the cowboys tried to ride through Indian lines to get the troops.

Well, every time one of the unfortunate people rode out of town, the enormous skunk would be waiting at the pass. He would be hunched down, his white stripe gleaming in the moonlight, and then he would rise up and spray the horse and rider with a force so powerful they would roll across the desert like tumbleweed. His spray had the force of a blast from a riot hose.

And then, once the people had been sprayed, they changed into mutants, hairy creatures with stripes down their backs. The first warning of the presence of one of these mutants was the pervasive odor of skunk.

"Do you smell what I smell?" the people of the town were always asking each other.

"It smells like . . ."

"Exactly what I was thinking."

The movie had been timed so perfectly that, as Mrs. Gray was saying, "That's all for today, class. Test on Friday," the enormous skunk and all the mutants were being attacked by crop dusters spraying a combination of Lysol and Ammoniated Top Job and Skunk-Away.

As Warren had gathered up his books, the people, transformed again into humans, were returning to their town. And as the skunk walked away from the camera, his tail high, in bright red letters appeared "The End."

Warren smiled. Maybe there were a few loopholes, but for a movie created entirely during first period, it wasn't bad.

In his goldfish movie, the police commissioner had sent an investigating committee into the sewer. There were three men on the committee, accompanied by a good-looking woman reporter who was after a story.

As the four made their way into the dark sewer, the reporter was saying into her tape recorder, "There is a damp stillness in the air, and there is a sense of something about to happen, or"—an uneasy pause, a glance around the creepy surroundings—"a sense of something that has already happened."

Deep within the sewer, Bubbles, who was sleeping in the slimy waters, awakened and stirred. In the short time she had been in the sewer, she had learned to sense when someone entered the sewer. It was the way a spider senses a victim approaching her web.

Slowly, her long golden tail curling deep in the

dark water, Bubbles let herself rise to the surface.

"I don't know why we have to spend a perfectly good Friday evening in the sewer!" one of the committee members was complaining. He shone his flashlight into the dark recesses. "We all know what's happened. The sewer workers have been in a bar for the past three days celebrating the World Series."

"But sir, there was a young girl." The reporter consulted her notes. "A Louise Otis. How do you account for her disappearance?"

"It wouldn't be the first time a young girl's gone off on her own. Do you know how many young girls run away every—" He broke off. "What's this? Look. A whole area here has been cleaned. It's strange; as if some very powerful force, a vacuum cleaner perhaps, ingested all the slime from this circle here."

"Yes, and here's another one."

They moved around the circles, skirting the clean spots because they might contain evidence. The girl reporter knelt and touched the inner circle.

She looked at her finger. "Not even a trace of dirt. Something very powerful has—"

"Has what?"

"I don't know."

In the awed silence that followed, one of the men said, "Listen, I've got to be at a Boy Scout Jamboree in an hour. Why don't we split up? We'll cover more ground. Let's meet back here in a half hour."

Warren loved it when people split up. "You go this way and I'll go that way" was when things really got scary, if a director knew what he was doing. And at this point Warren did.

The fat member of the committee in the Boy Scout uniform would get it first, he decided. The man was moving into the tunnel where Bubbles waited. As he rounded the bend he began to whistle a campfire song to keep up his spirits.

Below, Bubbles looked up through the murky water and caught sight of the formidable body moving along the side. The man's footsteps echoed through the tunnel. Three hundred and fifty pounds of food wrapped in a brown uniform. And Bubbles was hungry. She had not eaten in three days. Her fantail swished with silent power through the water. Her bulging eyes blinked—

Warren broke off, his head held to one side in thought. Did goldfish's eyes blink? Did goldfish have eyelids?

[68]

They would have to be very large eyelids—that was for sure—and Warren thought he would have noticed large eyelids. Still, he made a mental note to stop by the pet department at Woolworth's on the way home from school and check it out. He liked to be authentic.

Back in the sewer the fat man noticed something in the water—a swirling of golden color, veils turning below the surface.

He was curious. He moved to the edge, holding his light out over the water. He saw an enormous shadow below. He couldn't quite make it out. He leaned closer. He saw fins . . . eyes . . . a mouth. Why, it looked like a goldfish, but no goldfish could be that large. The thing had to weigh two thousand pounds!

He was now leaning over the water like one of the spectators at Sea World feeding the porpoises. He was just ready to call the others when suddenly the water was stirred by one enormous bubble. BLOOP! How interesting! The man—

"Warren!"

—went down on one knee to see better. And then the goldfish rose out of the water. The man's eyes popped. His mouth dropped open. He fell back on the seat of his Boy Scout uniform. His lantern clattered to the ground. There was an enormous slurping sound S-L-U-R-P and—

"Warren Otis!"

He looked up. His lips were still forming the word "slurp."

"Me?" He pointed to himself.

The movie had been so real, so vivid, that he had thought he was actually sitting in a theater. He was startled to see the classroom, the sun streaming in the window, the teacher moving down the aisle toward him.

"Yes, Warren, you."

"What is it, Mrs. Gray?" he managed to ask in a normal voice.

"I asked if you had finished your sentences."

"My what?"

"Your sentences—the sentences using your spelling words."

"Oh, no, not quite."

"Let me see what you've done."

She came back and stood by his desk. "You scared me," he explained weakly. "I slammed my notebook shut." He made a pretense of opening the notebook, turning through the pages.

There wasn't much to turn through. It was an old notebook of Weezie's, worn so thin on the corners that the cardboard showed through. He had fewer papers between his dividers than anybody in the class. "Well, it's here somewhere," he said. His face was beginning to burn.

"Try to find it, Warren," Mrs. Gray said. "It has to be turned in at the end of class."

"It will be."

As she moved to the front of the room, she said, "The reason I gave you this time to do your sentences, class, was so that you would have time tonight to watch the special 'The Origin of Language' on channel nine."

At the front of the room she turned. "If you aren't going to use the time to good advantage, well, then next time . . ."

As she trailed off Warren could feel students looking at him with open animosity. "Next time she gives us homework, it's his fault," a girl in the third row said, jerking her thumb in his direction.

"What page are we on?" Warren asked the boy beside him. The boy showed him. "Could I borrow your book for a minute?"

He turned to the girl on his other side. "Can I borrow a sheet of paper?" He liked to spread his borrowing around.

"Don't you ever have any paper?" she asked.

"I'm getting some this afternoon."

"I've heard that before." Disgusted, the girl ripped a sheet from her spiral notebook. Flecks of torn paper fluttered to the floor. "Here."

"Thanks."

With his eyes shifting rapidly from the spelling book to his paper, Warren began to write, carefully underlining each spelling word as he completed a sentence.

Try to be *sensible.*
Don't be *improper.*

He was lucky it was a list of adjectives. Even so, he knew his paper would be returned with a red zero at the top, but he didn't care.

Be *diligent.*
Never be *uninteresting.*

When the bell rang he sighed with relief. He had finished his last sentence. "Don't call others *ignorant.*" He put a period at the end and dropped the paper on Mrs. Gray's desk.

"I usually enjoy your sentences," Mrs. Gray said. "Sometimes they are very original."

"These are more like"—he paused—"like

rules." He gave her what he hoped was an appealing smile.

As he left the room his smile faded. Head lowered, he made his way through the shuffling, shoving crowd to Science.

"Things are quiet around here."
"Yeah, too quiet."

Warren stood in the pet department of Woolworth's, surrounded by the hum of gerbils on their exercise wheels, the cheep of birds in their cages. He was watching the goldfish. They did not have eyelids. He moved nearer, pressing his face so close to the aquarium that a mist formed on the glass from his breath.

You believe that you know everything about goldfish, he was thinking, staring intently at the fish, but there's always something to learn. He watched as one of the biggest goldfish, eyes bulging, fantail swirling, wiggled through the little oriental bridge at the bottom of the aquarium. His eyes lit with pleasure.

Maybe at the bottom of the sewer was some sort of old structure, and in the movie Bubbles could hide there, under the slime-strewn archway.

Suddenly Warren wished he had enough money to buy a goldfish. A goldfish of his own, he thought, would inspire him. And later, when he no longer needed inspiration, when the movie was over, he could—he smiled slightly—he could flush it into the sewer and into a new, fuller life of its own.

Warren blinked. He focused his eyes on the goldfish. It would be the first time he had ever had a miniature model of one of his movie monsters. He lifted his head, his eyes bright. "How much are the goldfish with the big eyes?" he asked the clerk.

"The Orientals? Seventy-nine."

"Oh."

She reached for the net to scoop one out. "Is there any particular one you'd like?"

Warren's hands opened and closed in his empty

pockets. "Seventy-nine cents is a little out of my price range," he said, using the phrase his grand-mother used when she was broke.

"The small ones are twenty-nine."

"I'll think about it." He wanted one of the big goldfish badly enough to steal it. He stepped back. However, stealing a goldfish was not practi-cal, he thought, unless a person had a long arm and a waterproof pocket.

He straightened, and with one final, regretful look at the aquarium, he walked past the garden tools and through the toy department to the front of the store.

Warren slowed as he passed the candy counter, eyeing the mounds of jelly beans, the pyramids of fudge squares. He stopped at the lighted case of nuts and inhaled the scent of warm grease.

Warren was hungry. All he had had for lunch was half of a bologna sandwich, a gift from his friend Eddie. And Eddie's gifts did not come cheaply. "You bring me a Twinkie tomorrow," he had said, his long, old-man's face as stern as a gangster's.

"I'll try," Warren had answered, as he always did.

He began to walk backward through the cosmetics, his eyes still on the candy counter. Goldfish and candy and Twinkies were all out of his price range today. Warren was broke.

There was a woman on the penny scale by the door, her eyes sadly watching the sweep hand rise to two hundred pounds. Warren slipped on just as she stepped off. He was good at getting his weight free. As usual, seventy-nine pounds. Warren was stalling for time. He did not want to go home.

He was still bitter over the fact that his grandmother had taken his postcards, had stepped on them like a crazed giant. She had had no right to do that. They were not her postcards. His bitterness was growing as the time to go home got closer.

He paused in the doorway of Woolworth's to put on his dark glasses. He wondered where his grandmother had hidden the postcards. He knew she hadn't destroyed them because his grandmother never got rid of anything. She was known for her collections—twenty-three bed pillows, seventeen perfume bottles, eleven miniature lamps. He himself sometimes felt like part of a disappointingly small collection when she said, "And this is Warren, one of my two grandchildren."

He walked the six blocks to the apartment slowly, lost in thought. His grandmother had probably hidden the postcards in the freezer compartment of the Frigidaire, he decided. She had folded them and stuffed them into an empty carton of green beans. That's where she kept her money.

He smiled to himself. His grandmother thought that was a big secret and always made Warren and Weezie step outside the kitchen when she got out her money, but the money she gave them was always cold, and this had led Warren straight to the freezer and the carton of green beans.

He went up the steps, stamping because his grandmother had asked him not to stamp, and knocked loudly at the apartment door. She had asked him not to do that too. "I'm home," he shouted. He waited with his lips set.

On the walk home his anger had grown. He was now determined to take up the argument with his grandmother. If she tried to avoid a fight by giving him the silent treatment, well, he would make her so mad by his behavior that she would have to fight.

When his grandmother did not come immediately to let him in, he knocked again, louder. "Grandma!" He kicked at the bottom of the door, and it rattled on its old hinges.

There was no answer. She was doing this on purpose, to spite him, he thought. That was why she hadn't gotten up this morning and fixed the sparse breakfast—oatmeal—she usually did. Or why she hadn't fixed his school lunch. He had intended to slam out of the apartment this morning, yelling, "I'm not hungry," but the plan had been ruined when she was not there offering him food.

He beat on the door with his fist. "Grandma!" He leaned his ear against the door. He could not hear the television. That was strange.

He straightened. Maybe his grandmother had gone out, but that would have been even stranger. She never went down the steps unless it was Sunday and she was going to Pepper's for her weekly visit. Even the time there had been a fire in the Oglesbys' apartment, she had waited at the head of the steps, not willing to take the stairs unless it was absolutely necessary.

"Send the firemen up when they get here," she

had called down the stairs to the departing tenants. "But if they carry me down, they have to carry me back up!"

"Grandma!" Warren shouted. He was yelling into the crack of the door now, tasting dust.

"Warren."

He glanced around. It was Mrs. Oglesby from across the hall.

"Yes'm?"

"Is your grandmother all right?"

He raised his shoulders and let them fall, startled for a moment out of his anger. "Why wouldn't she be all right?"

"Well, I went over this morning to borrow some coffee and there was no answer, and I went over after lunch and there was no answer, and I'm worried. I know your grandmother didn't go out because I can always hear her on the stairs."

Warren glanced at the apartment door as if seeking an answer there.

"I've got a key, but I don't like to use it unless it's an emergency. Well, now that you're here, we better go inside."

"Yes, I want to go in."

But as he stood there, shifting uneasily from one foot to the other, waiting for Mrs. Oglesby to get the key, he wasn't so sure. Lately he had developed a real dread of finding out things.

"Your grandmother has not looked well to me lately," Mrs. Oglesby said as she fitted the key into the lock. "She needs to have somebody looking after her instead of her looking . . ." She ended with a long look at Warren. The lock turned and the door opened. "There," she said.

Warren nodded. He tried to swallow the sudden lump in his throat, but it wouldn't go down. He took off his dark glasses.

He and Mrs. Oglesby walked together into the unlighted apartment. The shades were drawn, and the living room had a dim, unlived-in look. The stale smell of unstirred air filled his nostrils. The wicker rocker with the tied-on cushions, where his grandmother usually sat in the late afternoon, was empty.

"Grandma!"

Warren went down the hall. He paused to look in the kitchen. His grandmother did not believe in cleaning the kitchen until night, so usually by afternoon the counter was a clutter of coffee cups and dirty pots and pans. Today his grandmother had not even put the kettle on the stove.

The meaning of the old familiar phrases,

"Things are quiet around here." "Yeah, too quiet," really hit him. He felt the sort of dread he had only imagined before in his movies.

"This is her bedroom." He touched the doorknob. The door was closed as it had been when he left for school that morning.

"Gretchen?" Mrs. Oglesby called as she knocked on the door. "Gretchen?" She opened the door a crack, glanced in, and threw the door open wide. "Gretchen!" She crossed quickly to the bed, where Warren's grandmother lay in her bathrobe.

Mrs. Oglesby felt for a pulse. Over her shoulder she said, "Warren, go get Sam."

Warren inched into the room, drawn against his will to the sight of his grandmother, awkwardly arched over her collection of twenty-three pillows.

Mrs. Oglesby began throwing the pillows to the floor, getting them out of the way. Warren edged around the room, stumbling over the heater his grandmother used on cold nights. He stopped when he was against the closet door. He reached behind him and held on to the knob for support.

"Get Sam!"

"Is she alive?" he asked, choking on the words. He wet his dry, cracked lips.

Now that the pillows were out of the way and his grandmother was lying flat on her back, Mrs. Oglesby had her head on his grandmother's chest.

"Is she alive?"

Mrs. Oglesby raised her head. "Yes, she is alive. Now will you please go get Sam?"

"Yes'm."

Warren turned, and slipping slightly on the throw rug in the doorway, ran for the hall, shouting, "Mr. Oglesby, Mr. Oglesby, help!"

"No, no, you've got to take me with you. You can't leave me for the giant mongoose!"

"Farewell, my friend."

Warren was sitting on the sofa in the darkness. The door to the outside hall was open so that Warren would be able to see Mrs. Oglesby the moment she got back from the hospital. Even so, he got up every few minutes to peer over the banister at the empty stairs below.

Warren had wanted desperately to go with his grandmother in the ambulance to the hospital, but Mrs. Oglesby had been firm. "You wait here, and when your sister comes, the two of you can come over on the bus. You'll just be in the doctor's way."

"I've got to come!" He felt the sort of desperation a victim in his movies might feel when he was left behind as monster food. "No, no, you've got to take me with you. You can't leave me for the giant mongoose!"

"Farewell, my friend."

"Warren." She had put her hands on his shoulders, but he threw them off in one furious gesture.

"She's *my grandmother*!"

"Warren," she continued in her even, adult voice, "you can help your grandmother most by staying out of the way."

That was a terrible way to help somebody, he thought as he drew back, stunned, fighting tears. By staying out of the way! He had continued to stand in the same spot, listening to the struggles of the ambulance attendants on the stairs, then to the slam of the door, the silence, the long wail of the siren outside. Warren had never felt so alone in his life.

He thought he heard the door open downstairs. He got up quickly, ran out into the hall, and stared over the banister. There was no one there.

He leaned forward, resting on his elbows, his hands dangling over the railing. He sighed aloud.

If his grandmother died . . . He had to think about this possibility, he told himself, because of the terrible way his grandmother had looked when they were carrying her out on the stretcher. Pale, sort of grayish, her eyes open a little, half-moons of white showing, her jaw slack. He had never seen a dead person except on television or in the movies, but he was sure that was the way they looked. He felt goosebumps rise on his arm, remembering.

If his grandmother died . . . He straightened abruptly. His eyes snapped open. If his grandmother died, he went on in a rush, his mother would come home! She would have to! It was such an awesome truth it took his breath away.

He paused, holding tightly to the railing with both hands. In his mind he was already at the funeral. He could see the mourners, all in black. They would be standing together around the open grave, under black umbrellas—a light rain would be falling. And back in the mist, half hidden by the towering old tombstones, would be a lone figure, a black hat pulled low over her face, hiding her red hair.

"We are gathered here today," the minister would be saying in a low, sad voice.

He alone would have noticed the woman. He alone would know it was his mother. He would not be able to run to her, of course, even though that's what his whole body would be aching to do, because the FBI would probably be there, waiting for just such a move. But afterward, as the funeral procession was leaving, he would slip away and hide behind one of the tombstones.

The rest of the people, lost in grief, never even noticing he was not there, would climb into the long, black limousines, their voices floating back to him, and they would drive away through the old iron gates.

Warren would remain crouched behind the tombstone until the cemetery was empty and still, and then he would hear the sound he had been waiting for—the crunch of footsteps on the wet gravel. The footsteps would come closer, closer, would be at the very stone behind which he was crouching.

Warren would rise, straighten his shoulders, and there she would be—his mother. Her eyes would be swollen from crying. She would have taken off her hat, and her hair—the red color he remembered—would be blowing back from her pale face.

"Warren?" she would say in a puzzled voice, unable to believe this was happening at last.

"Yes, it's me."

And then his mother would hold out her arms in the way he had imagined so often, only this time it would be really happening. And he would run forward with a glad cry, and they would—

"Warren, why on earth are you standing out here in the hall crying?"

He spun around. It was Weezie. She had come up the stairs so quietly he had not heard her. He whipped the tears from his cheeks.

"What is wrong?"

He looked at her, as stunned for a moment as if he had been interrupted in the middle of one of his movies. Then his face collapsed as he began crying again, this time aloud.

"Grandma's gone to the hospital!"

"What? I can't understand you. Stop crying!"

"Grandma's gone to the hospital. Mrs. Oglesby thinks it's a stroke."

"Oh, no."

"Mrs. Oglesby said that her aunt looked exactly the same way and she d-died."

He turned his back, crying now out of guilt, ashamed he had wept earlier, not about his grandmother going to the hospital, as he should have, but over the joy of possibly seeing his mother again.

"Please don't cry, Warren."

"I can't help it."

"Grandma'll be all right. She's been to the hospital before. She's had attacks before."

"Not like this."

He dried his cheeks with his hands and then wiped his hands on his shirt. "We're supposed to come to the hospital on the bus. I wanted to go in the ambulance—" He began crying again—he couldn't help it. "But they wouldn't let me."

"Honey, I don't think they let people go in the ambulance. They work in there. They have oxygen and medicine, and half the time the people are better by the time they get to the—"

"They let Mrs. Oglesby ride up front," he interrupted stubbornly. The need to be part of his grandmother's illness swept over him again. If he could have gone with them, helped somehow, just handed them things—there had to be something he could have done.

"Warren, listen, we'll go in the apartment and

get some money. You wash your face."

He nodded dumbly.

"Then we'll go down and call Pepper—somebody ought to let her know—and then we'll go to the hospital in a cab. We are not waiting for any bus."

Warren sniffled loudly. He watched his sister with a grateful admiration as she went into the apartment. No, it was more than admiration. He felt close to Weezie for the first time in his life.

"The money's in the green-bean box in the freezer," he called after her.

"I know," she answered.

He followed slowly. He went into the bathroom and dried his face on a towel. His grandmother only bought brown towels because they never showed dirt. "You never have to wash them unless you want to," he could remember her saying as she hung them over the towel racks.

He felt the pinch of tears again, and he walked quickly into the living room. In the kitchen Weezie was slamming the freezer door, rattling paper. "Warren, you ready?" she called.

"Yes."

"Let's go."

She came out of the kitchen stuffing cold dollar

bills into her purse. She pushed him through the open door and paused to lock it.

"Weezie?" he asked.

"What?" She put the key in her purse and looked up, pausing to see if she had forgotten anything.

"If Grandma dies—"

Her eyes sharpened as she glanced down at him. "Grandma won't die."

"If she does though—"

"She is not going to die."

"But if, I'm just saying *if*!"

"All right, say it then. If what?" she asked, her voice rising in the empty hall.

"If she does die, will Mom come home?" he asked in a rush. Then he looked up at her, waiting, his eyes still bright from tears, his mouth open, for her answer. He did not even seem to be breathing.

"You never give up, do you?"

"Why do you say that?"

"You *never* give up."

He gritted his teeth. "All right, I never give up! So will she come?"

"No."

"What makes you say no? I think she would.

She would have to come home, wouldn't she, to the funeral?" He was squinting now as if the light had suddenly gotten too bright.

"No."

"She would!"

"No!"

"Well, maybe she wouldn't be right out there in front, but she would have to at least be there somewhere, wouldn't she? She would hear about the funeral. Somebody would tell her. And she would *have* to come. She couldn't stop herself. All right, maybe we wouldn't get to *talk* to her, but she would . . ."

Weezie was looking at him, shaking her head with such sadness that he trailed off.

"Come on, Warren," she said, starting down the steps. "Let's get to the hospital."

"She would have to!" He threw the words at her back. He waited, but she did not even turn around. Head lowered, he followed her down the steps.

"If I didn't know better, I'd think something metal was coming down the stairs. Well, it's probably nothing, but I'd better go check."

From the back, Warren thought, Aunt Pepper looked exactly like his mother. She was standing, peering into the square of glass on the door of the intensive care unit. Her long, reddish hair was pulled back with a barrette. Her foot was tapping impatiently on the worn tile floor.

The hospital was old. Warren glanced up. Across the high ceiling ran plumbing pipes, painted the same green as the walls and ceiling. Down the hall an elderly man was waiting in a wheelchair to be pushed to his room.

Warren and Weezie sat on straight chairs in the small waiting room. Weezie was holding a worn issue of *McCall's,* but she had not opened it.

Warren was concentrating on not thinking about his grandmother, because every time he thought about her—he could not help it—his mind jumped straight to the graveside and her funeral.

He was genuinely glad no one could read his mind. They would be shocked to discover that while everyone else was worrying about his grandmother's health and praying for her recovery, he was imagining meeting his mother at her funeral. He was shocked himself.

To change his thoughts he looked around the room. This hospital would not be a bad setting for a movie. Of course it would have to be abandoned, the halls unlighted, the small waiting room empty of furniture.

Perhaps some sort of radioactive creature could break into the deserted hospital, attracted by the pull of the old X-ray machines, needing a fix. It could be some sort of snakelike creature that would weave through the ceiling pipes and drop down on people.

The thought caused him to shudder, and instantly Weezie put her arm around him. "Are you all right?"

"I'm fine," he said. He shrugged off her comforting arm, which he knew he did not deserve.

"The doctor should be out soon."

"Good."

He rested his head on the back of the chair and looked up at the ceiling. Maybe the pipes themselves could come to life, he thought. That would be original.

Pipes coming alive didn't seem likely, of course, but his friend Eddie claimed he had once seen a horror movie about a car. A car came alive and went around running people down! Eddie swore it was the truth.

Convinced he was on the right track, Warren continued. The pipes would have been activated by old radioactive waste material that hospital officials had been illegally disposing of for years through the plumbing. Not bad, he thought.

It would have to be a very quick thing, sort of catch the audience by surprise. First one pipe would began to quiver—this would be the beginning of the movie—and then one length of the pipe would crack and snap off and fall to the floor.

In a sort of metallic frenzy, like a fit—the

viewer would just see a blur here—the pipe would undergo a transformation and grow a tail and a head. The mouth would be a zigzag line that snapped open and shut, the eyes would light up, and the tail would have rattles.

Killing these pipes would be next to impossible. Bullets would be out. Poisonous gas, useless. Dynamite would blast them into little pieces, but then the little pieces would activate and start snapping their jaws again. The best scientific brains in the nation would meet to—

But he was getting ahead of himself. Back to the beginning of the movie. One pipe would form into this snakelike creature, and then another and another until finally an army of pipe snakes would be upstairs in the hospital hall.

The night watchman would be the first to learn of their existence. He would be at his station, sipping a little booze, listening to the radio, when suddenly he would hear this terrible clattering noise echoing through the empty halls.

"If I didn't know better," he would mutter, getting slowly to his feet, "if I didn't know better, I'd think something metal was coming down the stairs. Well, it's probably nothing, but I'd better go check."

There would be alternating shots of the old night watchman climbing up the stairs and the pipes coming down. With each shot of the night watchman, the noise would be louder.

"What *is* that?" he would ask, more and more puzzled. He would shine his flashlight up the stairs, peering into the darkness.

Then he would see them, the pipe snakes, their jagged mouths snapping open and shut as they came clattering into view.

"No! No!"

Dropping his flashlight, he would turn and start running down the steps. He would trip on the third step and tumble head over heels to the bottom. There he would crouch with his arms over his head for protection.

"No! Please! No! Noooooooo!"

But the pipe snakes wouldn't kill the old man. Eating flesh wouldn't be their thing. They would just clatter right over him and around him and on down the steps and out the front door of the hospital.

In the silence that followed, the old man would get up like a cowhand after a stampede. He would brush himself off, check his arms and legs for injuries, pick up his flashlight, shine it around the empty stairs. He would shake his head in disbelief.

Then he would go to his station, pick up his half empty bottle of booze, and drop it into the nearest trash can. "Never again," he'd say.

Warren realized he was sitting there with a smile on his face. He looked around quickly to see if anyone had noticed. Aunt Pepper was still at the door. Weezie's head was turned the other way. The old man in the wheelchair had fallen asleep.

Film critics would call the movie "original" and "powerful." They would say, "Excellent special effects." He would like to see the movie himself—that was the real test of one of his movies, when he himself would pay money to see it.

There were, of course, problems to work out. For example, why would everybody be scared of the pipes if they didn't do anything but run around? Sure, nobody would want pipes running wild in the streets, cutting across yards, making holes in lawns. That would be a terrible nuisance.

Maybe the pipes could activate other pipes, make them leap right out of washing machines and toilets and join in the stampede. Housewives would see the pipes coming and go after them with brooms. "Stay away from my pipes!" POW! SWAT! ZONK!

Warren was smiling again. Quickly he put his hand over his mouth to hide his expression.

Weezie put her arm around him again. Her look was sympathetic. "Are you sure you're all right?"

"Yes." He pulled away, shrugged off her arm, and settled back into his thoughts.

Suddenly Weezie's look sharpened. "What are you thinking about?"

"Nothing."

"I would really like to know."

"Nothing! I'm not thinking about anything. What makes you think I'm thinking about something?"

"You don't have to be defensive."

"I'm not being defensive. I just wasn't thinking about anything. You want me to make something up? All right, I was thinking about school. Are you satisfied? Anyway, I was *not* daydreaming, if that's what you were getting at."

"You daydream too much."

"I said I was *not* daydreaming." He crossed his

arms and sat back in his chair, his mouth set, his eyes dark. He began to kick his heels against the chair legs.

"I can always tell when you're daydreaming because you have a sort of out-of-it look on your face. It's very obvious. It's like you're on drugs or something."

He snapped around and stared at her. "I suppose all your thoughts are perfect. I suppose you were sitting there thinking about world affairs!" He was so angry he was trembling.

"I was thinking about Grandma!"

"Sure you were!"

There was a pause and then Weezie said, "A little daydreaming is fine, Warren. It's like a little food or a little wine. Only when it becomes the most important thing you do, when you gorge yourself with food . . . There's a girl in my school who freaks out on food, and she's bigger than somebody in a sideshow. She's carried eating so far she can't even lead a normal life. And you're carrying daydreaming too far. You're a daydream freak. You're not in the world ninety-five percent of the time."

"I am," he sputtered. "I— It's not the same." The accusation was so unjust he could not find the right words. "You're stupid, you know that! And anyway, nobody in the whole world is going to tell me what to do with my thoughts. My head's mine, and—"

"Kids!" Aunt Pepper came over. "Be quiet. Honestly, you're disturbing people. You've got to keep your voices down."

"I wasn't the one who was yelling," Weezie said, adjusting a pleat in her skirt.

"You were the one who wasn't minding her own business!" Warren yelled.

"Kids!"

Aunt Pepper watched the two of them for a moment. She looked from Weezie's calm face to Warren's scarlet one. When she apparently was satisfied that the argument was over, she turned and crossed the room to the door.

"Anyway," Warren said through lips that barely moved, "did it ever occur to you that my thinking may turn out to be valuable? Did it ever occur to you that I might really make movies when I get big?" He swallowed. His eyes stung with tears of injustice. He had been creating a movie—he had been going to call it *Pipe Snakes!* —it was going to be a blockbuster. And his stupid sister had labeled that "daydreaming."

"Nobody does anything by daydreaming about it," she said. "You don't see successful men sitting around looking like this." She gazed down the hall with a blank look on her face. "There are people who like to do things and there are people who like to daydream about doing things. It's—"

"Mind your own business, hear? Just shut up."

"Kids!"

As Aunt Pepper moved toward them, the door behind her opened. "Mrs. Walker?" It was the doctor.

"I'm Mrs. Walker," Aunt Pepper said, spinning around. Weezie got to her feet.

"Well, apparently your mother has had a stroke. We won't know for a few days how much damage has been done. She's awake now, if you want to see her."

"I do."

"Your mother's a little confused, keeps calling for someone named Saffron—Saffee?" It was a question. He looked from one to the other.

It was Warren who answered. "Saffron's my mother."

"Well, perhaps she should come if she possibly can."

"That's what I was thinking," Warren said.

"Something is wrong."

"There generally is when the cattle are found with two holes in the sides of their necks."

"I don't know how you stand it without a telephone," Aunt Pepper said. She was pacing up and down the living room like an athlete ready for a race. "It just drives me crazy to think that someone might be trying to call me and because there's no phone— Aiiiiiiiii!" She shook her head in mock craziness. "Who in their right mind would be without a phone?"

For the two weeks that Warren's grandmother had been in the hospital, Aunt Pepper had been staying with Warren and Weezie.

Warren said, "You can use the Oglesbys' phone in an emergency."

"I have used the Oglesbys' phone so much that she has put up a sign—'Local Calls, Ten Cents'—with a little ashtray for me to put coins in. Anyway, I want my own phone. It's probably ringing right this minute." She broke off and said, "Doesn't Weezie have boyfriends? How does she get dates?"

"I don't think she has any."

"Of course she has boyfriends. Weezie's very pretty."

"She's too big. Some kids call her Hercules."

"She is very pretty. Doesn't she ever go out and you don't know where she's going?"

"Yes."

"Well, that is dating. 'Where have you been?' 'Nowhere.' 'Who are you going with?' 'Why do you want to know?' That person," Aunt Pepper said with a smile, "is dating!"

"When Weezie goes out like that—I mean secretly—well, I always think it has something to do with Mom."

Aunt Pepper turned and regarded him seriously. Warren was tired of being looked at like that.

He said, "I know what you're getting ready to say. I know!" He slumped. He began kicking his heels against the sofa.

"How do you know what I'm going to say when *I* don't know what I'm going to say?"

"It's just," he went on, "that there is so much I don't understand. Weezie's always saying things like, well, she says things like maybe I wouldn't want to find Mom, maybe I wouldn't like what I found. She tries to make me think there's something terribly wrong, that Mom's turned into some sort of monster!"

Aunt Pepper sighed. She sat down on the arm of the chair. "I think I know what's bothering Weezie."

"What?"

"Well, Weezie found out from her father—she went to see him a couple of Sundays ago—and she found out that your mother was here for three months last spring."

"Here? In this city?"

Pepper nodded. "She lived with some people in an apartment on the east side, and Weezie's dad saw her a couple of times and—"

"I don't believe it!"

"Honey, it's true. I wouldn't make up something like that. She—"

"If Mom had been here for even one day, she would have come to see me. I know she would."

"She did see you once or twice. She went to your school and watched you come out."

"What? Watched me come out of school? How would she know which one I was? How would she know when my room gets out? The third graders get out a half hour before us—did she think one of them was me?" He got to his feet and began walking around in circles. "How did she even know what school to go to? Why didn't she speak to me? There's a boy in my room that looks like me and people get us mixed up—maybe that was who she saw, maybe she spoke to him."

"Oh honey, stop it. Honey!"

He turned. "Did you see her?"

"Once."

"Where?"

"Well, she was waiting when I got off work. She was standing across the street by the newsstand, and we walked down the street and went into Albert's and had a beer. We talked and—"

"Why didn't she talk to *me*? Why didn't she take *me* somewhere?" He felt he had so many questions he would spend the rest of his life getting answers. "What did you talk about?"

"She wanted to know about you. She said she'd seen you. And, honey, she knew exactly which one you were. She knew immediately. She said you had on a navy jacket and dark glasses."

"A lot of kids wear dark glasses."

"And I told her you wanted to be a movie director and that—"

"Why did you tell her *that*? I didn't want her to know that."

"I told her because I knew she would be interested. And I told her about how you and Grandma come over every Sunday and how you and I talk. I told her you were original and funny and that she was missing out on a lot."

"And what did she say?"

"She said, 'I know that.' "

He sat down heavily. It was a rocking chair, his grandmother's, and he sat on the edge. He had thought when he was little that this was a magic rocking chair because it would never turn over. No matter how hard he rocked, and sometimes he would rock hard enough for the chair to balance for one scary moment on the tips of the rockers. Still, it never turned over.

Now the world had gone so wrong that if he leaned back even the slightest bit, the old chair would tip him onto the floor. He held on with both hands.

"Oh honey, your mom's gotten herself into such a mess. She's gotten in with real violent people. They're making bombs, and some of them have robbed banks, and—"

"Not my mom!"

"I think she wants to come home. She looks tired. She's thin. She's—"

"I don't even want her to come home now."

"You're just hurt because your mom was in town and you didn't get to see her, and I understand how you feel. It's all right if your mom's out in San Francisco and she really can't get to see you, but if she's *here*, well, it's so much worse."

"I used to go around when I was little, and I would want my mother so much that I would say it to myself over and over. 'I want my mom—I want my mom,' like that. And sometimes I would forget and say it out loud on the bus or at school. 'I want my mom!' like that. And kids would look at me like I was crazy. 'He wants his mommie. Warren wants his mommie. Warren wants his mommie,' and I would sit there with tears in—"

"What are you two sitting in the dark for?" Weezie opened the door to the apartment with a bang and snapped on the overhead light. "There."

"We were talking about your mom," Aunt Pepper said. She spoke as carefully as she used to say her lines on television. "About how she was in the city for a few months last spring."

Weezie let her books drop onto the end table. "And did not bother to see us."

"She saw you, Weezie, she—"

"Oh yes, she stood on the school steps—or she *says* she stood on the school steps—and watched for our faces in the crowd. There are, may I point out, thirty-four hundred students in my high school, so she would have to be very quick."

"She saw you," Pepper said. "She described you perfectly—your hair, your clothes . . ."

"Oh, all right, maybe she saw us. But that makes me even madder. She saw us, probably for about thirty seconds, and then she went away feeling all wonderful and satisfied, probably motherly. 'I have seen my children. They looked so happy. They looked so healthy.' That's what she said about us, isn't it?"

Aunt Pepper didn't answer, just watched her with sharp eyes.

"Isn't it?"

"She felt better after she saw you, yes."

"And so off she goes feeling better, without a backward glance. Without once thinking that Warren and me might want to feel better too. We could use a little satisfaction ourselves. I wanted to see my mother! Warren wanted to see her! And yet the only thing that mattered to her was *her* satisfaction, *her* feelings."

There was a knock at the door. "I'm sorry to interrupt," Mrs. Oglesby said, sticking her head inside, "but there's a call from the hospital.

"I'm coming," Aunt Pepper said. She got up and started for the door in one motion. "We'll finish this later, Weezie," she said over her shoulder.

Weezie and Warren remained where they were—Weezie beside the end table, Warren holding tightly to the arms of the rocker.

"Something's wrong," Weezie said in the sudden silence. "I know it."

Warren did not answer. There had never been a moment this filled with dread even in his movies. Often actors had said, "Something is wrong," and it always sent a chill of pleasure up his spine. And it was always followed by something even more chilling. "There generally is when the cattle are found with two holes in the sides of their necks."

Waiting for something bad to happen was one of the pleasantest parts of a movie, like waiting to go over the top of a roller coaster was the best part of the ride.

There was no excitement in this, sitting on a rocking chair that had begun to tremble because he himself was trembling.

He glanced over at Weezie. She was looking down at her school books, lifting the cover of her English book, letting it fall.

They heard Aunt Pepper coming back from the Oglesby apartment. Warren got up from his chair so suddenly that it rocked back and forth like a chair taken over by an invisible spirit.

Aunt Pepper came in and leaned against the wall. "Grandma's dead," she said.

"It looks human, Professor, but underneath that human exterior, there is something not quite . . ."

"Not quite what? Human, perhaps?"

"Exactly."

There were twenty people at Warren's grandmother's funeral, and they all sat on folding chairs under the green mortuary awning.

It was unlike any movie funeral Warren had ever attended because the day was beautiful, there was not a cloud in the sky, nobody had on black, and nobody was weeping.

Warren sat between Weezie and Aunt Pepper. He did not bother to search the cemetery for his mother because the cemetery was flat, and there were no tombstones for her to hide behind, just modern flat markers that a lawn mower could ride over.

As Warren looked around, he felt he could see miles of graves, with only plastic flower arrangements sticking up to break the view.

It seemed to Warren that modern society was doing away with all the good movie settings. They flattened cemeteries and turned swamps into housing developments and built sewage disposal plants. Soon there would be nowhere mysterious for creatures like Bubbles to live.

He closed his eyes. The main reason he was not looking for his mother was because he knew she would not bother to come.

"Let us pray," the minister said.

Warren bowed his head, but he did not close his eyes. There was a picture of his grandmother on the coffin, and he couldn't stop looking at it. In the picture his grandmother was slim and had black wavy hair and dark lipstick. She was smiling into the camera.

To Warren, it was as strange as seeing a picture of a young Santa Claus; Santa Claus with a lean body and black hair and a little moustache. Both pictures would have been snapped so long ago Santa and his grandmother would not have had time to develop their characters.

Warren was ashamed that he did not feel sadder. He had felt terrible that first night. He could not sleep because death seemed to hang over the whole apartment like smog, keeping out all good feelings. He had twisted and shifted, but there had been no comfortable spot, even in his own familiar bed.

He had started feeling better the moment his aunt Ginger arrived from Las Vegas for the funeral. She and Pepper were like girls when they got together.

"Oh, I have got to tell you this," Ginger would say, and Warren would draw close, like a dog to a fire. "I was singing in a little club in Frisco—very little, ten tables—and I look across the room, and there is Willie Leon Mantinelli who used to be in love with you in ninth grade."

"Don't tell me, let me guess. He was still short and fat, and he had bad breath."

"No, no, he was gorgeous, gorgeous, so gorgeous I didn't recognize him."

Warren would sit speechless, watching them, looking from one to the other. He could never remember there being laughter and stories in the apartment.

"He was tall—"

"He couldn't be tall. He came up to there on me." Aunt Pepper gave a light chop to her throat.

"Remember, men didn't wear high heels back then. Straight white teeth—"

"Come on! His nickname used to be Beaver."

"—curly hair, mustache, gorgeous! He comes over—his shirt is open, hairy chest, necklace—and he says his name is Bill. I say, 'Hi, I'm Ginger.' He is looking at me with interest, and I am looking at him the same way."

"Did his pimples clear up?"

"Yes, I tell you the man is gorgeous! He is so good-looking that I start thinking he must be somebody famous, on TV or something, and finally I say, 'Do you mind telling me your last name?' And he says, 'No, it's Mantinelli.'

"I had just taken a sip of red wine, and I spit it out all over him. I said, 'Aren't you Willie Leon Mantinelli, and didn't you go to Madison High, and weren't you in love with my sister Pepper all through ninth grade?' "

"Ginger!"

"And the poor man, before my very eyes, suddenly becomes short, fat Willie Leon. All the gorgeousness was gone, and he got up and literally ran from the club. The last I saw of him was his high heels tottering through the swinging door."

Sometimes Warren wanted to break into the stories and ask, "Did Mom know him too? Was Mom in on that?" but he didn't want to take a chance on being sent out of the room.

He tried to imagine his mother sitting cross-legged on the bed, laughing with her sisters, talking about old times, and it seemed to him as he sat there that knowing you could never sit and laugh with your sisters would be one of the worst things about being a fugitive. He wondered if years from now he and Weezie would sit together and laugh at the past.

"Let us pray," the minister said.

It must be a second prayer, Warren thought, because his head was still bowed from the first one. He looked up at the minister through his eyelashes.

Suddenly he noticed a figure in the distance, over by some trees. The figure hadn't been there before. His head snapped up. He drew in a breath so loudly his aunt Pepper glanced at him.

He started to get to his feet. "Warren." Aunt Pepper reached over and patted his leg. "Sit down, hon." She tried to press him back into his seat.

He remained in a crouch. The figure had long red hair! The face was turned away, but the long hair, pulled back in a ponytail, was his mother's hair.

"Warren." Aunt Pepper was pulling at his pants now. "Sit down."

He reached out, and clutched Aunt Pepper's hand. He squeezed it hard. He said, "It's her," beneath his breath.

"Who?"

"It's—"

He did not finish because the figure turned around then, and it was not his mother. It was a man with a red beard. He was holding a shovel. Warren realized it was a workman who was waiting in the trees for the funeral to end so he could come over and shovel the earth back into the hole.

"Are you all right?"

"Yes."

He sank back into his chair. He bowed his head, not knowing if the others were still praying or not. Tears filled his eyes, and he began to bite the insides of his cheeks so he wouldn't cry. Just once, he thought as he bit harder, just once he would like to cry for the right reasons.

"Ashes to ashes, dust to dust," the minister was saying.

The sounds of his own sobs surprised Warren. He had burst out crying the way volcanoes erupt. He could feel people looking at him in quick sympathy. He tried to close his mouth, to choke back the sobs, but they only burst forth louder. He could barely hear the words of the minister now.

"—watch over you and keep you and bring you peace. Amen."

"It's over, hon."

Warren was the first person to get to his feet. He rose so quickly that his folding chair tipped over backward and snapped shut over the artificial grass that covered the mound of dirt. He bent to pick it up.

"Honey, everything's going to be all right," Aunt Pepper took him by the shoulders and turned him around to face her. "You've got me. I'm going to move in with you and Weezie, and we're going to fix up the apartment. This isn't the end of the world. Don't cry. Please."

"I can't help it." He swallowed, straightened

and then bowed his head as one final burst of sobs came out. "I'm sorry. I can't help it. It's just that . . ." He did not finish. He could not tell. He wept into his hands.

The minister put one arm around his shoulder. "Come and see me if you want to talk, son."

"I will."

Warren was the center of attention now. Everyone was stepping forward to comfort him. Ginger and Pepper had their arms around him. The old fingers of his grandmother's gin rummy club tapped him on the head.

He tried to twist away. It was like a scene in one of those old monster movies, he thought, and the monster is trying to get away from the peasants, to get back to his hiding place. The monster twists, turns, struggles and finally is caught and carried to a laboratory cage. The scientists peer at him through the bars.

"It looks human, Professor, but underneath that human exterior, there is something not quite . . ."

"Not quite what? Human, perhaps?"

"Exactly."

Yes, exactly, Warren thought. And with his head bowed he followed his aunts and sister down the path to the waiting cars.

"There's nothing that can stop the monster now. His growth cells have gone wild!"

The neighborhood dog pack of two was making its way down the sidewalk. The yellow dog had a bread wrapper in his mouth, and the spotted one was rubbing against him, trying to dislodge the package and get one of the pieces of green bread inside.

The only person in sight at the moment was Weezie. Warren was hiding in a doorway. He was following his sister, slipping after her like a spy, hiding in shadows, dodging behind buildings.

After supper Weezie had said, "I'm going out,"

and when the door closed behind her, Warren was on his feet instantly, pulling on his own jacket.

"Me too," he called to Aunt Pepper. She was in his grandmother's room, painting the walls white. The room seemed large without his grandmother's clutter. Her combs and brushes, her collection of perfume bottles, her china señorita doll with the lace mantilla, her pillows, her plastic-flower arrangements were all packed away. Only her coat hangers clicked together in the empty closet.

It was the first Monday of the month, and all of them knew Weezie was going to the pay telephone in front of the library to wait for a call from their mother.

"Good luck," Pepper called as the door closed.

"Right."

Now Warren peered around the doorway of the dry cleaner's. When he saw that Weezie had turned the corner, he ran to the store on the corner and stopped. He peered around the dingy window.

Weezie was standing there, hands on her hips, waiting for him. "Why are you playing this ridiculous game?"

His mouth dropped open. "What?"

"Why are you pretending that I don't know you're back there? You're about as subtle as a freight train, you know that? I can hear you running and then stopping. When you were hiding behind the mailbox I could hear you breathing."

"I didn't want you to try to make me go home. I've got as much right to talk to Mom as you have."

"I wasn't going to make you go home. I should have brought you a long time ago. You've built up too many dreams around Mom."

He felt the urge to protest rising inside him the way it always did when Weezie accused him of idolizing their mother. This time he swallowed it down and said, "I know."

"So come on. We'll miss the call if we're not there right at seven. *If* there is a call. Sometimes it doesn't happen, you know. I stood in that phone booth in a snowstorm for two hours last January."

"Why didn't you just leave after fifteen minutes? That's what I'd do."

"Because I thought, well, maybe she is on the coast, in another time zone, and she's forgotten, so she'll call at seven *her* time and that will be— oh, never mind. Anyway, phone booths are colder than refrigerators; believe me. I know."

Warren walked along beside his sister, feeling a strong bond with her. For the first time he found he was matching her long strides, keeping up with her. This was probably why soldiers kept in step—so they would feel unified.

"You better plan what you're going to say, though," Weezie said, interrupting his thoughts. "Sometimes Mom only has enough money for three minutes."

"Oh." Warren had not thought of this. He stumbled over a crack in the sidewalk. "What are you planning to say?"

"Well, first I'm going to tell her about Grandma."

"Good." Warren did not want "Grandma's dead," to be the first words he spoke to his mother in three years. "I'll go last."

"All right."

As he walked, he imagined Weezie saying, "Mom, Warren's here. He wants to talk now." He imagined taking the cold receiver in his warm hand—his palms were already getting sweaty—and leaning close. "Mom?"

That was as far as his imagination took him. What would he say then? he wondered. What could he say that would be interesting?

His thoughts raced through the last three years of his life: a broken tooth—he ran his tongue over it—almost getting run over by a school bus, his friend Larry moving to Chicago—she didn't even know he had had a friend named Larry—getting that miraculous A+ on an English test.

He shook his head. These were things you told your mother every day when you got home from school, things you told at the kitchen table while you were having cookies and milk. Tonight he had to tell his mother something so interesting, so fascinating she would not want to hang up even when the call was over.

His main interest, of course, was his movies, but that would not do. He would need at least a half hour to do justice to one of those.

And then, right in the best part—something like "There's nothing that can stop the monster now. His growth cells have gone wild!"—right in the middle of something like that, she would say, "Well, I have to hang up now. Bye-bye." Click.

"What sort of things do you usually say?" he asked carefully, looking up at his sister.

"Oh, I tell things about me, about the family.

Sometimes she asks questions. Sometimes I do. There's never enough time, though."

"Oh."

They rounded the corner and there was the library. In front, the phone booth was lit up. It was the only thing Warren saw. It dominated all the important buildings. Indeed, the buildings did not even seem real, a painted backdrop.

Suddenly Warren cried, "Weezie there's somebody inside." He ran forward a few steps. "Look, somebody's in the booth talking!" His voice broke with disappointment and frustration. He turned to his sister.

"We've still got"—she looked at her watch calmly—"three minutes. If he's not out by then, I'll declare an emergency."

Warren had begun to wring his hands. They were so slick with sweat that it was as if he were washing them with soap.

"Weezie!"

"Look, don't worry about it. It's not the first time I've had to evict somebody. One time I stopped a lady in the middle of giving a recipe."

"But what if he won't—what if you can't—"

"I'll get him out."

Suddenly it seemed to him that Weezie was the

strong one, the Wonder Woman, the person who could save the world. At any rate, he knew she would save this moment, and that was all that really mattered.

He looked up at his sister. He was dazzled by the glowing picture of her yanking the man out of the booth as the library clock struck seven, tossing him across the street, stepping in just as the phone began to ring, saying coolly, "Hello."

Warren had always thought a person had to do big, overblown things to be great. And yet this—Weezie getting a man out of a phone booth so they could talk to their mother—this was the most heroic feat he could imagine.

They walked together to the phone booth and stood outside the door. Inside, the man was saying, "Let me explain, Marsha, I can explain it if you'll just give me a chance."

"What time is it now?" Warren asked, shifting nervously from one foot to the other.

Weezie looked down at her watch and held up two fingers. Warren waited without speaking. With her eyes on her wristwatch Weezie waited, then she held up one finger.

"Get him out," Warren said.

She nodded and knocked on the door of the

booth. The door rattled loudly, and the man glanced over his shoulder in irritation.

"We have to use the phone. I'm sorry. It's an emergency," Weezie said. She sounded like a policewoman, Warren thought proudly.

"What? This is a public phone. I'm in the middle of a conversation."

"I'm sorry. Are you aware of the penalty for refusing to give up the phone in case of an emergency call?" She paused, added, "Two hundred dollars or thirty days in jail."

"What?"

Weezie did not answer. The man glanced at the phone in his hand, up at Weezie's stern face—she was taller than he. "All right, lady!" He said quickly, "I'll call you right back," just as Weezie took the phone from him and hung it up.

"We won't be long," she said.

"Well, how long? I've got other calls to make. I've got to—"

"Three minutes."

The man moved outside and sat on the library steps, watching them. He glanced down at his own watch.

Weezie let out her breath in a long sigh of relief and stepped into the phone booth. She waited with her head lifted, her hands resting on the ledge just below the phone. In the open door Warren watched her, knowing she had stood like this so often it was a ritual, like something a person does in church.

"I thought this was an emergency," the man called from the steps. "Aren't you going to make your call? There's probably a penalty for pretending to have an emergency when you—"

Weezie lifted one hand to shut him up.

It was then that the phone rang. Warren reached out and gripped the sides of the booth for support. Weezie waited for the second ring. Then she lifted the receiver.

"This is Weezie."

Warren watched. He saw Weezie's face relax. "Hello, Mom." She turned to Warren and included him in the moment. "It's her," she said.

"Folks, I've called you together because our town has a little problem."

"I wouldn't call being buried under a thousand feet of leaves a little problem."

Warren was breathing through his open mouth, and his throat was getting so dry he didn't think he would be able to speak when his turn came.

He shifted uneasily. His brow wrinkled with a troubling thought. *If* his turn came.

"Well, Grandma had a stroke," Weezie was saying, "and she was in the hospital about ten days . . . no, she was conscious, she asked for us, for you." Weezie had not paused once since she began talking. She was going on as if she had all evening to talk. "No, Ginger didn't get here while Grandma was in the hospital, but she came for the funeral. She's still here . . . no, Pepper's moving into our apartment. She's painting Grandma's room tonight. It feels so funny to see it empty."

Warren pulled at Weezie's coat sleeve. She moved her arm away. Her expression was intent. Warren pulled at her sleeve again. Weezie shrugged him off. It was as if she were trying to rid herself of a fly or a mosquito.

"In a minute," she said irritably. Into the phone she added quickly, "No, nothing's wrong, Mom. It's just Warren. He wants to talk when I'm through. Only let me finish about Grandma. She—"

The man on the library steps called, "Three minutes are up," in a nasty voice.

Warren was gripped by panic. "Weezie!" he cried. His knees had begun to tremble. "Let me have a turn." He tried to get into the booth with her, but she turned her back and blocked his way.

"Weezie!" He felt Weezie had gone crazy, like one of those hysterical people who really intends to give up the gun or the telephone and then loses control and can't. She needed to have cold water thrown in her face or be slapped, neither of which he could manage.

He reached for the phone. She pulled it out of reach, but not before he got his finger in the cord. "Gimme!" He yanked.

"Warrrennnnnnn."

As she turned he dived in, and then they were in the phone booth together. Warren's head was crammed between the side of the booth and Weezie's shoulder. "Let me—" he began.

Then he heard a faint voice say, "Weezie, are you there? What's happening?"

Warren gasped. It was his mother, the first time he had heard her voice in three years. He stopped struggling.

"It's me, Mom," he yelled, his face turned to the side, shining. "It's Warren."

"Warren."

It was like an echo, a word spoken years ago and only now reaching him.

He struggled to get his head out from under Weezie's shoulder. "Let me have a turn, Weezie," he begged, but her hold was as firm as a wrestler's.

"Oh, pumpkin." Now his mother's voice was as he remembered it. "How are you?"

[131]

He had to swallow before he could speak and then, throat cleared, all he could say was, "I'm fine."

The operator cut in and said, "Your three minutes are up."

"Wait. Wait. I'll get more change." There was a flurry of sounds as his mother begged some people for quarters. With a sigh Weezie released Warren and moved the phone down, holding it between them so they could both hear.

"There, seventy-five cents." They heard the coins clang through the machinery. "Kids?"

"We're still here," Weezie said.

"Warren?"

"Me too."

Then a silence came on both telephones. Warren didn't want to say anything because he was afraid he might start speaking at the same time as his mother. He waited, turning his eyes from Weezie to the silent phone.

Finally Weezie broke the silence. "Mom?"

"I'm here."

Warren realized from the way his mother said it that she had started to cry. He wrapped his arms around himself, tucking his hands in his armpits.

He was somehow glad that he was not the one holding the phone.

"Don't cry, Mom," Weezie said.

"I'm not. I think I'm getting a cold. I just wish I could have been there when Mom asked for me, that's all. I wish I had known. I wish I had been with you at the funeral. I wish . . ." She was unable to finish.

"Mom, you could not have done one single thing."

"I know, but . . ."

She trailed off. Warren knew she was crying again. He looked up at Weezie. Tears were flowing down her cheeks too. Her earrings were trembling.

"I have to go," his mother said, her voice far away and fading. He wondered if the connection had gone bad. "I can't talk anymore."

"Don't hang up yet," Weezie said. "Listen, Mom, we're all fine. We're all right. Don't worry about us. Don't cry."

"Yes, we're fine," Warren chimed in, feeling far away and fading himself.

"Take care of yourselves."

"We will," Warren said.

"Don't hang up. I'm not through. Mom—"

"Be good. I'll talk to you soon." Warren could barely make out the words. It was like the last rushed lines on her postcards. "I'll write. I love you. Good-bye."

"Good-bye!" he called.

"Mom!" Weezie shouted, but they heard the click, the sound of the broken connection. Weezie hung up the phone as if it had suddenly gotten heavy. "She's gone," she said.

"Yes."

They stepped out of the booth and stood for a moment, feeling the chill in the air.

"It's about time," the man said as he brushed past them. "That was over four minutes." He closed the door behind him, took out his dime.

"It didn't seem like four minutes to me," Warren said. He put his hands in his pockets. He felt the key to their apartment—the first key he had ever been allowed to have. His grandmother had always said, "You don't need a key. I'm here to let you in," but Aunt Pepper had a different idea. "We're all in this together. We're all equal." His fingers curled around the piece of metal.

"Well, you've had your first talk with Mom," Weezie said.

[134]

He took out his key and looked at it. He wondered why there was comfort in a piece of metal that would open a door. "Yes."

In the phone booth the man said, "It was an emergency, Marsha. Some kids. I had to hang up."

"Let's sit down for a minute, want to, Weezie? I just don't feel like going back right now."

"All right."

They walked to the little park beside the library and sat on the first bench. Warren looked up at the high, arched windows and the stacks of books that gave the illusion of going from the basement to the roof.

"You know," Weezie said, "I have never, not once, I have *never* talked to Mom and felt better when I hung up the phone. Either I feel bad for her or I feel bad for me."

"I know," he answered. Even though he had only had the one conversation, he understood that was the way it would always be.

"And I *never* get to say all I want, ask all I want. Tonight I wanted to ask about all those weeks when she was here, right in this city, and she didn't contact us. I wanted to say, 'Why?' " She shrugged. "Only I didn't get the chance."

"Because she started crying."

The leaves were beginning to fall from the park trees, and a sudden gust of wind sent a shower of golden leaves swirling down on them.

Warren glanced up. He thought he and Weezie would soon be covered with leaves. There were so many. He could almost smell the clean autumn smell of a pile of leaves.

It was, he thought, like one of those moments in his horror movies when some perfectly natural event of nature occurs: the appearance of a single spider, a single snail, a single rock sliding down a cliff; and then the gradual increase, the single spider becomes a dozen, a hundred, thousands, the rockslide pours down the mountain; and the mayor finally has to say, "Folks, I've called you together because our town has a little problem."

"I wouldn't call being buried under a thousand feet of leaves a little problem."

The wind stopped, and the last leaves fluttered to the path before them. Warren looked over at his sister. At one time he would have been excited over the thought of a mountain of leaves. At one time he would actually have taken pleasure in a leaf disaster, in seeing in his mind the city grind to a terrible halt.

No more. He was glad that trouble was over for one evening. He had had enough. It was all he could do to handle everyday problems.

Weezie turned up her collar. "Are you ready to go?"

He nodded. He got up, and kicking the leaves into a flurry of gold, he followed his sister out of the park.

"Son, tell the listeners how it feels to see your very own two-thousand-pound goldfish, your little— Do you remember what you called her?"

"Bubbles."

"—to see your little Bubbles killed in front of your very eyes."

"It feels awful."

Maybe I won't daydream quite so much," Warren said as they walked home. He was thoughtful. "Maybe it isn't good for me." He glanced at Weezie to see if she was going to congratulate him on a mature decision, but she was staring straight ahead, lost in thoughts of her own.

Warren felt as if he had just poked a toe into water to test it, and it was not as cold as he thought it would be. Still, no need to plunge in all at once, he thought.

"However," he went on, talking more to himself than to his sister, "I suppose it would be all right for me to finish the one I'm on."

"Are you talking about your movies?"

"Yes."

"Sure, finish the one you're on. You want me to listen?"

"Well, this movie's about a two-thousand-pound goldfish that's down in the sewer." He paused. Weezie was looking at him blankly. "You know, the sewer, under the city. The goldfish got so big from a chemical called XX-109 that was being dumped into the sewer."

"Go on."

"Well anyway, at this point it has just been learned that the goldfish is responsible for the deaths of five innocent people—no, six. Two sewer workers and—"

Warren broke off as he remembered that Weezie herself had been the third victim. "And some other people," he finished lamely.

"Go on."

"Oh, never mind. It'll be quicker if I tell it to myself." Suddenly he actually wanted to get it over with. He could never remember feeling like this before.

"I don't mind listening."

[139]

"No."

Suddenly it occurred to Warren that his movies were best when he wasn't sharing them with another person. He couldn't bear looks of boredom. He didn't think he could stand to go into a theater full of people watching, say, *Goldfish!*, and see them looking at his work of art as indifferently as Weezie.

Well, he wasn't bored. Things were popping in the sewer. A group of policemen and soldiers were making their way inside. They were armed with rifles, bazookas, and flares. Walkie-talkies were crackling with messages.

Far below, in the dark-green water which reflected the searchlights, Bubbles sensed that the sewer had been invaded. The vibrations that came to her through the trembling water were bad, and she did not rise to the surface to investigate. She remained in the deepest recess of the sewer, a huge, golden shadow, her lidless eyes watching, waiting.

The soldiers were marching side by side with the policemen. The tramping of their boots echoed along the walls. Suddenly their way was blocked by a small boy with dark glasses on his head.

Warren did not usually take roles in his own movies, but this—his last—would be an exception. And this time he would be the hero. He squared his shoulders beneath his jacket.

He would stand bravely in front of the men, holding out his thin arms, blocking the way, looking even smaller in the harsh lights.

"Step out of the way, son."

"But it's Bubbles. It's my goldfish. You can't kill her!"

"Out of the way."

"You can't kill her. You can't. I won't let you!" But his tiny boyish arms would be useless against grown men and guns. He would be thrust aside.

As the men tramped past his crumpled body, moving deeper into the sewer, a reporter would kneel and ask, "Now, what's all this about, son? The goldfish is yours, you say?"

"Yes."

"How do you know?"

"Well, I flushed her down the toilet one Tuesday last year and—"

"Son, millions of people flushed goldfish down the toilet last year. My own mother—"

"And now," he would go on, interrupting, "even though she has been changed into a two-

[141]

thousand-pound mutant by a material called XX-109, she is still my goldfish. I would know her anywhere. It's the eyes."

"Ladies and gentlemen, this young boy is the owner of the goldfish which the soldiers and policemen are going to attempt to annihilate."

"They can't kill her. They can't! It's not her fault. It's the XX-109."

"Son, tell the listeners how it feels to see your very own two-thousand-pound goldfish, your little— Do you remember what you called her?"

"Bubbles."

"—to see your little Bubbles killed in front of your very eyes."

"It feels awful."

"Go ahead and cry—here, this way, toward the camera. All the viewers are with you. They've all had goldfish. They know what it's like to flush one down the toilet. If there's anything we can do—well, I know the folks out there would like to help, and—"

"There may be one thing."

"What?"

"Well, sir, I've been thinking about it, and I believe that if every single person in this city flushed their toilets at, say, ten o'clock, well,

I believe the sewer would be flooded with water—"

"I get it! The floodgates would be forced open, and Bubbles would be washed out to sea!"

"Yes, where she could live the rest of her life in peace and harmony."

"It might work. Sam, get a camera out by the floodgates, just in case. This is a long shot, but . . . Folks, do you want to save Bubbles, this boy's two-thousand-pound goldfish? Do you want to prevent Bubbles from being shot like a dog? If you do, I'm asking each and every one of you to get up out of your chairs right now and to go to your bathrooms. Don't say, 'I'll get up during the commercial.' Don't say, 'I'll do it in a minute.' That may be too late.

"I'm starting the countdown, folks. It's *five* minutes to ten. If you have more than one bathroom, get a neighbor to come over and flush with you. Let's all get in those bathrooms. Put down your knitting. Put down your newspapers. Close your refrigerator door. You can eat later.

"It's *four* minutes to ten. I'm asking every single person within the sound of my voice to help us. This is an emergency. I'm asking you to call a neighbor, call in a pedestrian off the street. Open your windows, yell, 'Flush at ten o'clock,' to the people in the streets below.

"It's now *three* minutes to ten. Parents, call up your kids. Kids, call your parents. If your husband's at work, give him a call. Secretaries, tell your bosses. You bus drivers, stop your buses and let your fares go find rest rooms.

"It's now *two* minutes to ten. Every single one of you ought to now be within reach of a commode. Every single one of you ought to be reaching out your hand, grabbing a flusher. Don't jump the gun now. I don't want to hear any toilets pre-flushing.

"It's *one* minute to ten. Just one minute to go, folks. Let's count together. Twenty-nine seconds . . . twenty-eight. Remember, we need every single one of you. This little boy is counting on you. Bubbles is counting on you. Nineteen . . . eighteen . . . seventeen. Folks, don't let an innocent goldfish pay for the crimes of society. Twelve . . . eleven . . . ten. Get ready, everybody. Count with me. Let's hear it! Seven! Six! Five! Four! Three! Two! One! *Flush!*"

An enormous spate of water would roar into the sewer, carried by every pipe in the county.

The policemen and soldiers would come running out.

"It's flooding!"

"The sewer's a wall of water!"

"The floodgates are bursting!"

"Run for high ground!"

And as people scattered, it would happen. Like water crashing through a dam, an enormous wave would gush down the spillway, sending foam as high as buildings, crashing through the waterway, a green wave so awesome people miles away would hear its boom and wonder.

And just under the crest of the enormous wave could be seen, for a fleeting second, a flash of gold, the swirl of a long, graceful fantail, the fleeting wisp of a golden veil, the curve of an unlidded eye.

And then the wave would empty into the sea with a roar, creating more waves that would shake boats and rattle docks and circle back and crash against the rocky shore.

And then silence.

"We'll never be troubled by a two-thousand-pound goldfish again."

"That's for sure."

Well, I guess she's gone," the chief of police
would say as he watched the receding water.
"Bubbles is on her own now."

"It's a big ocean, Chief. I reckon there's room
for all God's creatures."

"We'll never be troubled by a two-thousand-
pound goldfish again."

"That's for sure."

And then the reporter would turn back to the
boy. "Son, tell the folks how it feels to save

the life of your very own two-thousand-pound goldfish."

"It feels great! And I'd like to thank all the thousands of people who helped. It was their flushing that really saved Bubbles."

"That's right. Bubbles owes her life to the fine men and women of this city. And, I might add, to the fine plumbing.

"Well, folks, that's all for now. This is Rick Watson for WMTV, saying, so long, folks, and thanks for flushing."

The camera would travel back into the sewer to get a final shot of the excited crowd, framed in the archway of the entrance. The water would be rising again in the sewer, and, outside, the sounds of the shouts and glad cries would grow fainter as the music swelled—an entire orchestra of strings. And then, at that moment, rolling up onto the screen in huge, orange, oriental-looking letters, would come—

THE END

Warren sighed with total satisfaction. He glanced at his sister. What a wonderful movie to end on, he thought. He wished now he had told it to Weezie. He had not known it was going to be such a masterpiece.

He stumbled slightly and reached out for Weezie's arm to keep from falling.

"You all right?" she asked.

"Yes," he said quickly.

The reason he had stumbled was because in the depth of the sewer—hidden from the reporter and the chief of police, and the people —clinging to the long green slime of the sewer wall, shining, glistening, was one huge, perfect, golden egg.

Warren himself had only seen it for a second. The camera had flashed by so quickly, and then, of course, the water was rising, bubbling over it.

Still, he knew what he had seen. Before Bubbles had been flushed out to sea, she had laid an egg. And the egg was as big as a Volkswagen, so the goldfish inside was not going to be one of your twenty-nine-cent-Woolworth's varieties.

He glanced guiltily at his sister. He didn't want her to suspect he had already started *Goldfish II!* And right after swearing off daydreams.

He shook his head to clear it of unwanted sights and sounds. It was hard to shake off a way of life, though. He realized that. It was going to be hard to get that single shimmering, glistening egg out of his mind.

At least he now thought he saw the big pitfall of daydreams. You dreamed, say, that your mom would come home for your grandmother's funeral. And then came the hard, cold reality—the real funeral—and your mom didn't come, and you ended up without a grandmother that you were only beginning to realize you missed.

He made a solemn vow that if he did break down and create a new movie, he was not going to waste the lives of people he knew in them. I will not waste family and friends, he said to himself—they are hard to come by.

He turned back to Weezie. "You know, I don't feel as bad as I did before. I'm glad I got to at least hear Mom's voice."

"Sure, well, it's always better to have unhappy communication, I guess, than no communication at all."

"Only, Weezie, next time, you've got to let me talk. You wouldn't have even let me say, 'Hello,' if I hadn't forced you to."

"I don't know what came over me. It was just like I was—"

[149]

"Crazy," he supplied.

"I guess. But all I have of Mom is three minutes a month. And that's when I'm lucky, when she calls. Three lousy minutes, and it is the hardest thing in the world to share it."

"I know."

"We're just going to have to get used to the fact that you and I are probably going to have the worst fights ever staged in that phone booth."

He watched her for a moment, and then he said, "Weezie?"

"What?"

"Do you ever daydream?"

"Sure."

"What about?"

"Well, I do not daydream about two-thousand-pound goldfish." She grinned down at him.

"I really want to know."

"Well, when I was your age I used to dream about becoming a lawyer, and Mom would be on trial for something, and I would get her off."

"What do you dream about now?"

"Just that I will become a lawyer."

"Weezie, you're going to be a lawyer?"

"Yes."

"You never told me that."

"I never told you because you wouldn't appreciate it."

"No, no, I do." He could see her in his mind at court, bigger than the judge, than the opposing lawyers, her head sticking up like a mountain poking up through the clouds. It was such a vivid picture that he stopped walking and stared at her. "Weezie, you're going to be a lawyer!"

"I know. Now, will you come on? I promised Aunt Pepper I'd help her paint."

"I'll help too." He kept staring at her. He had never thought of Weezie as a lawyer before, but now he saw that it was perfect.

"I get the roller because I can reach higher than you and Aunt Pepper," she said.

"A lawyer!" he said as he followed her.

"Yes, a lawyer."

"I get it. That's why you study all the time."

"That's why."

"Hey, maybe you *will* defend Mom some day. Maybe something will happen. She'll—"

"That," she said, pointing at him, "is my daydream. You make up your own."

"I did, but I'm finished now."

He paused on the curb while Weezie stepped into the street, watching for traffic. To fill the emptiness of not having a daydream, he allowed the actor to repeat "We'll never be troubled by a two-thousand-pound goldfish again."

He heard the other actor answer, "That's for sure."

Somehow it didn't seem quite as satisfying as Weezie's dream. He almost felt like an amateur. He watched his sister with sudden envy.

Anyway, nothing's for sure, he said to himself, remembering that fleeting glimpse of the golden egg. He glanced down at the drain at his feet. He smiled slightly. Then, shaking his head, he followed his sister across the street. "Wait for me," he called.

About the Author

Betsy Byars was born in Charlotte, North Carolina, and now lives in South Carolina where her husband is a professor at Clemson University. They are the parents of three daughters and a son.

Mrs. Byars is the author of many books for children. Among them, *The Summer of the Swans* which was awarded the Newbery Medal in 1971, and *The Pinballs*, which has received numerous honors, and was the basis of a popular ABC Afterschool Special. *The Pinballs* is available in an Apple® Paperback edition from Scholastic along with *Trouble River, Goodbye, Chicken Little, The TV Kid* and *The Cybil War*.